the BLUE GIRL

the Blue Girl

A NOVEL

LAURIE FOOS

COFFEE HOUSE PRESS :: 2015

COVER DESIGN by Linda Koutsky

AUTHOR PHOTO © Miriam Berkley

Coffee House Press books are available to the trade through our primary distributor, Consortium Book Sales & Distribution, cbsd.com or (800) 283-3572. For personal orders, catalogs, or other information, write to: info@coffeehousepress.org. Coffee House Press is a nonprofit literary publishing house. Support from private foundations, corporate giving programs, government programs, and generous individuals helps make the publication of our books possible. We gratefully acknowledge their support in detail in the back of this book.
Visit us at coffeehousepress.org.

LIBRARY OF CONGRESS CATALOGING-IN-PUBLICATION DATA

Foos, Laurie, 1966-
The blue girl / Laurie Foos
pages cm
ISBN 978-1-56689-399-2
I. Title.

PS3556.O564B59 2015
813'.54—DC23

PRINTED IN THE UNITED STATES

FIRST EDITION | FIRST PRINTING

ACKNOWLEDGMENTS

Sections of this book have previously appeared in *Solstice: A Magazine of Diverse Voices*, the *Rake*, and *Wreckage of Reason: An Anthology of Contemporary XXperimental Prose by Women Writers*. "Moon Pies," an excerpt, was awarded second place for the Calvino Prize in 2007.

for Ella and Zachariah,

and

in memory of my mother, Anna Foos

Irene

THE BLUE GIRL EATS SECRETS IN MOON PIES. SHE takes them in, her mouth and lips smudged white against her blue skin, tongue clacking at the roof of her mouth, crumbs dribbling down her chin. We present them to her in the quiet of her room while she lies beneath the old, pitted, gray comforter and sucks in ragged breaths. Slowly her eyes close as we pass our secrets across the bed and into her hands. We watch as she swallows them, sometimes whole, sometimes in excruciating bits. Sometimes, when the old woman who lets us into the house draws near, the girl gasps or twists her mouth, but mostly she seems to enjoy them, her lips pursed with the sticky surprise of the things we have come to offer her, the things that she has come to take.

The old woman just opens the door to the girl's bedroom and lets us in, one at a time. Magda is first, and then Libby always last, and I am in the middle, because it doesn't matter to me when I go in since it was my daughter, Audrey, who saved her, on that day she almost drowned, that day that everything changed.

She breathes in her quiet way when I feed her the moon pies—moon pies that are never store bought, the ones it takes so much time to bake, to press pieces of my life into round cakes filled with sweet marshmallow cream that occasionally sticks in her throat. She smiles at me when she is finished, and on days when I am brave, I reach forward and wipe her lips with a handkerchief that I keep hidden beneath my wallet and lipstick, empty gum wrappers and tissues—the things that mothers my age so often carry with them.

She began eating our secrets after that first time she tried to drown. It was not something we had expected she might do. We did not know where she had come from, what her name was, or why she was blue. We still don't. Some of us have theories. There are whispers that the families who come to summer in the cottages can hear her wheezing through the trees that surround the lake. Some people say that her breath keeps them awake at night, but I never hear it, not even when all the windows are open and I lie in bed listening.

Some say she swallowed a bottle of Drano when she was a child, and that the poison that raged in her throat left her speechless and blue. But none of us knows why her skin remains mottled and bruised, why she doesn't burn in the sun like the other girls in town, why she doesn't speak to any of us. We do not know who the old woman is, and we know the blue girl will never tell. We do not know her name, not even now, after we have offered her our secrets and watched her swallow them whole.

The day she almost drowned we went out to the lake. It was the end of summer, just after Labor Day and before the first day of school, when the cottage people had finally packed up and gone. Magda and Libby and I had piled our teenage girls into our cars and had driven out to enjoy the lake without the crush of all those summer mothers and their children who left food and toys in the sand, and their husbands who drank too much beer and often came only on weekends.

I'd left my son, Buck, at home, even though he begged to come, hopped up and down and screamed at me in a voice I'd never heard. Perhaps, we thought, that if we saw the blue girl in the lake as it was rumored that the summer people had, we might come to know her, though even then I think we realized that knowing her was not going to be possible.

That day on the lake the sun raged and blistered our

daughters, each of them fifteen and seeming to want to burst free of their bathing suits: my Audrey, Magda's Caroline, and Libby's striking Rebecca. We kept them close to us on the beach towels and watched them slather themselves in oil. They sprayed their hair with lemon juice and smiled at each other but never at us. Their faces turned pink from sunshine, pink as with new life. We sat in a row at the shoreline and looked down at our freckled arms, the three of us squinting even under the heavy straw hats we wore to protect us. We were vain then and did not want wrinkles to drive our husbands further away from us, men who already shrank away when we reached for them, shrank at the feel of the stubble on what had once been smooth armpits and creamy thighs. We did not want our daughters to suffer these indignities. We wanted more for them.

We sat with our daughters at the beach, each of us with sons at home who could be unruly, especially Libby's poor Ethan, eighteen and unmanageable, with his flat ears and eyes that did not focus. We sat with our daughters, free of the sons who so often drained us, and at first we didn't see the blue girl. Our daughters jumped up and pointed at her swimming along the horizon, out past the buoys, but still we did not see. Audrey glared at me and turned her face away from mine, as she'd been doing for so long, and I pulled my hat down low over my brow and tilted the umbrella to shade her.

The daughters had been leaning together, whispering, when the blue girl began to thrash. At first the water foamed above her, white sparks flying in the air like tiny geysers, but then the water seemed to open up and amass itself into a glittering whole. Someone screamed, and our sunhats blew off our heads, our cellophaned sandwiches kicked by the wind.

That girl is drowning! someone shrieked, a woman's voice, and at first I thought it came from one of the summer mothers who always seemed to be accompanied by a gaggle of little girls in striped bikinis.

The girl! came the scream. *The girl out there is drowning!*

I looked around for one of the cottage mothers who had lagged behind, one of those with an accent unlike ours, with a husband who did not watch his children. Only then did I realize the scream had come from Magda. One of the daughters screamed, and yet we did not move. We did not throw off our sunhats, our glasses, and our caution to save her.

Only Audrey, my Audrey, ran to the water's edge before I could say or do something to keep her with me. She leaped into the lake, diving into the space where the rocks below the water lurked, and swam with her arms flying and water sputtering from her lips to grab the girl's arms and drag her to the water's edge.

The girl was lying on her back in the sand, and we stood above her, staring down at her motionless blue body turning bluer with every second that passed. We covered her body in shadow, as if this were the one thing we knew how to do. I felt the sun burning my arms as Audrey pressed her ear to the blue girl's lips and said in a flat, accusing voice, *She's not breathing.*

We said nothing. We, the mothers of these young girls, did nothing to help her. We simply stood and waited as Audrey pounded on the girl's chest, over and over, her hands slamming into the jutting rib cage. We, who had failed so many times, in so many ways, failed to help the blue girl return to life.

Slowly, Audrey turned the girl on her side, the swirls of veins and blood pooling in her bare arms and back, and clapped her between the shoulder blades, once, twice, three times, and still no sounds came from her lips, no breath surged in her lungs. Our daughters said, *Do something, do something,* but we did not, we could not. We did not want to touch her, not then, as much as she fascinated us with her blue hands and chest, the blueness now darkening all over.

Even then I knew that Audrey was not afraid of her, as Magda and Libby and I and most of the others in our small town had been. We watched, hovering, as Audrey fitted her mouth over the blue girl's lips and blew air into her lungs. We held our breath until she opened her eyes, looked up at us standing above her, and sighed.

Take her home, someone said—Libby, I think it was—even though we did not then know where she lived. Magda and Libby fled in their minivans, with their daughters strapped in the passenger seats next to them, while Audrey dragged the blue girl into the back of our station wagon and sat holding her hand. Even then I wanted to caution Audrey not to clasp her hand too tightly, since we did not know where this blueness originated. I feared infection, the girl's odd blue skin leaking into my daughter's flesh, soaking it with—poison? I looked back at them in the rearview mirror and tried to speak, but Audrey said under her breath, *Don't, just don't,* and I stayed quiet the entire drive, not sure where I was going or how I might get us back. I heard Audrey's whispers and the slush of the girl's breath, and I turned when Audrey told me to, passing the school and the liquor stores and the traffic lights that remained green even though I wished that they would turn red and make us stop. If we could just remain still for a minute, I thought, I could turn in my seat and see my daughter's face as it had been when she was nine, before she began to hate me, before this blue girl had come to town and almost drowned before our eyes.

Somehow Audrey knew where she lived. For a long time my friends and I had wondered where the girl had come from, where she and her family—if there was a family—had taken up residence. Some of us in the town had tried to find her at night at one time or another, but in the darkness she had always eluded us. We always seemed to lose her at the town limits, and each time, breathing anxiously in our cars, we decided to go home. But obviously Audrey had been successful, I realized, as we turned down a wooded road I'd never driven down in all the years we had lived there. The trees leaned in as if to encompass us, and when I looked up through the sunroof, I couldn't see the sun through the heavy branches, no matter how hard I strained.

When we reached the end of the road, I stopped and turned off the ignition, but then for some reason I started the car again, at the sound of her wheezing. Audrey didn't seem to notice. She opened the back door, took the girl's hand, and walked her up a gravel road that led to a house I could make out only in shadows.

Wait for me here, Audrey said, and I nodded slipping on my sunglasses. She did not look back at me as she drew the girl close to her side, her arm about the bony waist, and lumbered toward a grove of trees in the distance. I saw Audrey limping from the feel of gravel stabbing at the bottoms of her bare feet, and I leaned out the window, wanting to call to her to take her shoes, to tell her that the soles of her feet would tear, but I knew she would not listen, and so I did not speak.

I sat in the car and stared into the space where the trees met and watched my daughter move beyond the trees, the white stripes of her bathing suit disappearing. I closed my eyes and listened to the whir of the motor, trying to block the memory of the gurgle of breath that had come from the girl's mouth. I could still hear that breath, even as I held my hands over my ears to block out the sound.

I knew I should not have let my daughter go into that house alone, that I should have been there beside her as she presented the girl to whomever was there to claim her. It should have been me that the girl huddled against, not my fifteen-year-old daughter who knew so little of the world and yet had done what I'd been unable to do.

We no longer speak of the day the blue girl almost drowned. Now that the children have gone back to school, Magda and Libby and I drive out to the lake on Tuesday nights, after the children have gone to sleep, after our husbands have come home and eaten the dinners we have so adequately prepared. Nothing seems out of place, we make sure of that. Magda bakes chicken cordon bleu, Libby steams rice with vegetables, and I roll meatballs and simmer the sauce that Buck loves to let drip from his mouth. Some nights Audrey takes her dinner to her room and watches television in the dark, because we can no longer turn on the television in the living room. In July, when the lake still swarmed with summer people, my husband, Colin, decided the television was about to explode and sat crouched in front of it for three weeks. There had been a flash one night from the screen, a signal that scrambled, and Colin screamed that we were all in danger. Even when we turned the television off, he could not be convinced. When he could not get up from his crash position, I called the ambulance, and Buck and Audrey watched their father get taken away. Now he does little but play games of imaginary basketball. He throws a Nerf ball that once belonged to Buck at a hoop screwed to the top of the door frame. We leave the television off, as we promised him we'd do.

Colin no longer speaks to any of us. I know I should talk to Audrey about her father's endless games of imaginary basketball, about her friends, about the blue girl, about the troubles I know she is carrying, but I also know better than to press her. And so, on Tuesday nights I wrap the moon pies in aluminum foil and tell myself that I will be able to save my daughter—that I will be able to save all of us—once all the secrets have been eaten, digested, and somehow done away with.

On the nights that we go to visit the blue girl, we leave our cars parked on the side of the road and walk through the dark woods without flashlights. We have found that we prefer the darkness. On this night, Magda pulls up ahead of me and turns her headlights off, while I open my car door slowly, listening to the crinkling of the aluminum foil in my hands. Magda wraps hers in a linen napkin that she leaves at the foot of the girl's bed. I hear Magda's footsteps coming toward me and meet her at the edge of the road, where we wait for Libby, who is always the last to arrive.

The smell of the marshmallow cream is overpowering. I kiss Magda's cheek in the dark and ask her if she smells it, too.

Yes, she says. *This time I used a whole can.*

I sigh and lean against her. We never speak of the secrets, only the moon pies we have made, and even then, we are careful not to reveal too much. I talk to no one about Colin or the television, the hospital ward and medication, the games he now plays in the living room. We do not talk about Magda's son Greg and Libby's Rebecca, who have begun to sneak away in the night and touch each other in the spaces we have only recently forgotten. And of course we do not talk about Ethan, Libby's son who speaks in a strange voice and is bussed to a school outside of town. Magda's secret tonight seems to be an important one, a large one. Even in the dark I can tell that Magda has been crying.

Libby arrives before we can say anything more, and I offer Magda the handkerchief from my purse and hold it out to her. She takes it and wipes her eyes as we listen to Libby's footsteps in the grass. We take each other's arms and head up the gravel road to the house. A rock embeds itself in my shoe, and I feel it moving along my bare toes, pressing in between and rubbing, but I close my eyes against the pain and continue to walk. When we are almost at the house, Libby stops and sniffs. I am thinking of her son, of Ethan, who must smell the pies and want them. I wonder how she keeps him away.

Oh my God, she says, *how much cream did you two use?*

I feel the rock dislodge itself as I shake my foot.

Magda sighs and says, *Don't even ask.*

Libby sneezes, as the smell of the filling covers us in a cloud. All at once we begin to laugh, covering our mouths to muffle the sound. I feel the laughter hiccup in my chest and then explode. It has been so long since I last laughed, I'm afraid I won't be able to stop.

When we finally quiet ourselves again, we walk, the gravel crunching under our feet. The air is cool now that summer is gone, and I wish that I'd brought a sweater to drape around my arms and shoulders, something to protect me from the chill I always feel when we approach the door.

It is Libby who knocks. We do not know how this was decided, but that first time we visited with moon pies in our tote bags, Libby was the one who had nerve enough to knock. It makes sense to me that she would be the one, that she would have the courage to summon, since she not only has the prettiest girl in town, the girl that all the locals want to touch, but also the son who rocks back-and-forth, who flings himself down on the floor, who is still so very much a child. She knocks softly, so softly it is almost impossible to hear it. Before any of us can think about knocking again, the door opens, and we step inside.

The house is dark, as always, and the old woman stands in her stocking feet on the threadbare rug. She looks up at us through her thick glasses and rubs her hands together, then nods to each of us, one at a time, and allows us in. She stands looking at us for a long time and then signals Magda toward the bedroom, leading her in while Libby and I stifle coughs from the stench of vanilla she has left in her wake.

Two chairs await us in the sitting room near the door that we came in, but we do not sit, even though the old woman pats a cushion. We shake our heads and refuse with tight smiles. The old woman shrugs, disappearing into a dark hallway that none of us has ever ventured down.

Magda is gone a long time. At first we hear only the creaking of the old floorboards in the house. There are no pictures on the walls, no cheerful flowers in vases, just the two chairs and the rug we stand on. I look around at the walls, and when I cannot look around anymore, I glance at my watch, but it is too dark to read the numbers. Libby nudges me toward the door to the girl's room. We step closer and wait.

It is then that we hear the blue girl's breath. It sounds like the water shooting up on the beach sand that day, the water that Audrey pounded out of her lungs. The sloshing grows louder, a sucking of breath and then nothing. A long choking gasp hangs in the air.

I hold one of the moon pies in my hand and look frantically at Libby, who drops her moon pie on the floor and runs toward the door.

No, no, I whisper. *Don't go in there, not yet,* but Libby is almost at the door, and I have to grab her by the arm to stop her.

She's choking, she says, and I tell her Magda will handle it, trying to move her back with me to the doorway, back toward the chairs and the rug and the way out.

As I back away from the door, I feel something squish under my left foot. I lean down in the darkness and pick it up, feeling the creamy filling in my hand, feeling Libby's secrets seeping out.

Don't touch it! she says, but it is too late. The marshmallow cream sticks in my fingers. Libby wipes it away with a ball of tissues.

I'm sorry, I'm sorry, I whisper.

She takes her fingers and pokes the moon pie back together, wrapping it back up in the napkin and holding it close to her breast.

When Magda comes out of the door, she says nothing. The choking has stopped, but the smell of vanilla fills the room. Magda heads out the door before we can say anything, and we sense the girl appear in the opposite doorway in her nightgown. We turn and see a smile broaden across her face. She sighs and points toward me, her finger glowing in the darkness, her whole face shining as if emitting its own light. I look back at Libby one last time as I feel her fingers close around mine, the filling squishing between our hands. The girl climbs into the bed and opens her mouth wide, wider than I have ever seen any mouth open. Her lips and tongue are blue, and she smiles as I begin to feed her, slowly at first and then faster as she opens her mouth so wide that her jaw clicks.

She swallows hungrily, and when the last crumb is gone, she motions toward my fingers. I shake my head and move to get up, but she reaches out and closes her fist over my hand and motions toward her mouth.

That's all there is, I whisper. *There is no more.*

These are the first words I have ever spoken to her. She tilts her head toward mine and leans forward on the bed, her nightgown slipping to reveal the blue pools in her chest, blotches that disappear into the stitching. She takes my hand and moves it toward her mouth, and before I can stop her, she is licking my fingers, her tongue twirling around my knuckle and then lapping at my palm. Her tongue is quick, darting in and out, and when I finally pull away, she sighs and leans back against the bed.

My hand is clean. All the way home, after waiting for Libby and walking back down the dark path to our cars, all I can think is how clean my hand feels, that never have I felt so clean.

Audrey

In my whole life I'd never seen anyone like her, this girl who showed up a few months ago, with skin so blue you could almost see through it and hair that looked like lightning bolts. Well, not lightning bolts exactly, but her hair made me think of lightning bolts, the way it curled at the top and wound around itself and then jutted out the sides of her head, as if she just dove down into the water and shook out her hair.

Now when I see her, I don't know what to look at first, her skin or her hair, which also looks blue even though I know it's not. Actually it looks like hair that's been stripped of all color, the way dark brunettes have to have their hair stripped before becoming blond. Her skin isn't a pretty blue, it's a strange blue, unnatural, not like the sky at twilight or deep like a cartoon, but glowing. It's as if she lights up somehow, like a house you pass at night when the shades are drawn. You start to imagine what the people inside are like, whether they're watching sitcoms or wanting to kill each other, and you see that flash against the blinds coming from the TV screen. *That's what she is,* I think, *a Technicolor blue that lights and flashes when no one is looking.*

Me, I'm always looking, can't stop looking, though I wish I could, I really do. It's not that I meant to follow her that night in August, a few weeks after they took my father away, then brought him back to where he seemed to be slowly going crazy. All I wanted to do was walk. I'd been sitting in that house for weeks where my dad stayed up all night in the living room and played his imaginary basketball games and watched the blank TV screen. All I wanted to do was get away. I didn't know how long it would take me, and really, I didn't care. Five miles is about how long it is from here to the lake. I guess I could have taken his car keys. He'd taken me out a few times to drive, but looking at the keys sitting there on the end table next to the TV set, always turned off the way it was, I decided I'd rather walk all night than take those keys. Those keys were just about all he had left.

At the beginning of the summer Rebecca turned beautiful, or maybe she was beautiful all the time and suddenly we all noticed. Greg noticed—Caroline's older brother—and now the two of them sneak off at night and do things to each other out by the lake and sometimes, even, at Greg's house after they think Caroline is asleep. Sometimes Caroline tells me about the sounds they make and imitates them, but I always tell her to stop, because when I hear about Rebecca making those sounds it makes me feel sad, thinking about her brother making his own strange sounds while rocking back-and-forth. And then there's my dad, who almost sounds like he's crying, or like a dog whimpering because you've shut him out of your room—sounds that made me start walking in the first place.

I must have walked for an hour, maybe more, and I got as far as the trees when I saw her coming out of the lake. An old woman held her by the hand and was dragging her back toward a house, a little house I'd never seen before, and having grown up in this town, I thought I'd seen them all. I didn't go any closer—not that night, anyway. I moved back, up toward the road and away from them, the girl soaking wet, the old woman pulling her by the hand. I couldn't hear what the woman was saying to her, and I've since tried to piece it together—something about the water and being good, something about food and not eating—but I don't know for sure what she said. Then for just a second or two, they stopped in the gravel and looked toward the road where I was hiding in the trees. Suddenly a spot of light hit them while I stood, with the smell of the woods and the lake all around me, and I saw that it was her, the girl they'd all been talking about, blue, and standing just a few yards away in her soaked nightgown.

I didn't get home until just before the sun came up, and I didn't see her again until that day out at the lake. I thought I must have been mistaken, that I hadn't really seen a blue girl. I'd almost forgotten her when the day came, the day she started to drown and I jumped in. It was nothing I'd planned to do.

Now, at night, with my eyes closed, when I smell the little cookie pies my mother is baking in the kitchen, the inside of my eyelids look blue. It's like she inhabits me. I shake my head against the pillow and quietly breathe, *Get out, blue girl, get out of my head,* but she won't go, she can't go. So now I never sleep. Of course I must sleep for a few minutes at a time, because otherwise I wouldn't keep on living. Or I'd go crazy like my dad. And one thing I do know: I am not crazy and I won't ever be.

I wake up with creases under my eyes and blue circles around the sides of my nose. Sometimes I think about telling someone I can't sleep anymore, ever, but then I know they'll start with the questions—questions about my dad and his games, questions about what it felt like to save the blue girl that day at the lake. If there's one thing I don't want, it's questions. I just know they'll be able to tell that I'm thinking about her, and I don't want anyone to know that, not my teachers and definitely not my mother, who keeps looking at me and asking, *Did you get any sleep last night?*

I want to say, *Do you see these blue circles under my eyes?* but since the day the girl almost drowned, I've never said the word blue to my mother. Ever. Even if she were to ask, *What color are your eyes?* I wouldn't say, *Blue,* not even then. Anyway, she's my mother, she knows what color my eyes are. If she didn't, what kind of mother would she be?

I let Buck ask me about the blue girl because he's only eight years old. He listens when he shouldn't, but he knows what he knows, so I'll answer Buck.

Since the day I saved her the only one who seems to care is Buck. No one else cares that she stopped breathing and practically died right there at the lake, and now she just lives in the woods as if nothing happened, as if she never came close to drowning, as if she wasn't even blue. A couple of times the guys at school have talked about going out there and finding her, but it's just talk. They're afraid of her. I'm not. I was a little afraid, maybe, that first time I saw her, that night when the light hit her. But not since I had my mouth over her warm blue mouth and then, later, when I walked her back up to that little house in the woods.

I don't know why I saved her. I didn't really have time to think about it. I just jumped into the water—which, as usual, was freezing cold—and pulled her out. I've always hated that lake, and now I just hate it more. The summer people ruin it with all their blow-up toys for their bratty kids and their barbecues and their lawn chairs spread out all over the sand like they own the beach. They come in with their big SUVs and their city accents, and they look at us like aren't we so quaint, and they call us townies when they think we aren't listening. After the blue girl came, I stopped caring so much about the summer people. I have other things to think about now. Now when I close my eyes I can still feel how warm her mouth was when I blew into it. And the skin was warm. Who would think skin like that would be warm?

At night Buck comes in my room and, as usual, asks me to tell the story again, about the day I saved her. He's only eight, and you'd think the story would scare him, but he gets this big smile on his face whenever I talk about her and doesn't stop smiling until he falls asleep. He doesn't like Dad's basketball games with the little hoop and the Nerf ball—I know that much because he told me.

Tell me about her, he said one night when I tried to talk about Dad and the TV and how we can never watch it anymore because it's just too upsetting for Dad. *Not about him.*

I think if I keep telling him the story about the blue girl, maybe he'll feel better about Dad and his games, and then maybe he'll get tired of hearing about her, too. But he never does. And the truth is, I haven't gotten tired of telling him about her.

One night when I couldn't sleep, Buck told me about a dream he had where the blue girl came to him and danced with a bag of sugar on his head. My mother uses sugar in those pies of hers, the chocolate ones with the marshmallow filling that she thinks we don't know about, the ones she says she's making for the bake sales at school. She thinks Buck and I don't know about the pies, but we do. We keep that between us.

Buck made me sit on the edge of my bed while he imitated the dance she'd done in his dream with the sugar balanced on top of his head. He was wearing his pajamas with sailboats and they seemed like they were dancing in the water as he danced on my rug, moving his feet forward, to the side, and then back, and then forward and side and back again.

Who taught you to waltz? I asked him.

He just smiled and said, *Shhh, you'll make me lose count,* and then he held his arms out in front of him as if he was holding a woman, and he waltzed all the way around my room.

When he finished he asked me if I liked his dream, and I said that I couldn't like anyone else's dream—no one could. Most of the time we don't even understand our own dreams—didn't he know that?

Most people don't like their own dreams, Buck. You'll learn that soon enough, I said.

He put the bag of sugar down on my bedside table and asked if he could lie down with me. I told him he had to promise to put the sugar back in the pantry where Mom keeps the rest of the stuff she uses for those pies: the bags of chocolate and the bottle of vanilla and the cans of marshmallow cream. He grabbed the sugar and ran out the door, holding it out in front of him as if the bag was contaminated. A few minutes later he came back, his face flushed. I rolled over on my side and made room for him in the bed next to me. Looking at the little sailboats all over his pajamas, I started thinking about Dad's basketball games, and the television in the living room.

Do you think we'll ever get to turn it on again? he asked. I told him I didn't know, but there was a small TV in my room, and he could watch that if he wanted to.

No, thanks, he said. *It's not the same,* and of course he was right.

We could hear Dad's feet on the carpet, and the ping of the wire hanger when he must have missed a shot.

Don't those sailboats ever make you seasick? I asked. Mom doesn't think of these things. Me, if I have a kid someday, I'll think about whether too many sailboats would make *my* kid seasick, I know I will. And if my kid doesn't like sailboats, I won't make him wear them.

Don't tell Mom but I hate these pajamas, they itch, he whispered. *I like the color on the sailboats though, because they remind me of you-know-who.*

When he put his head down on the pillow next to mine, his hair smelled like the lake.

Tell me one more time, he said, as I switched off the light. *I like when you tell me about her in the dark.*

So I told him, again.

I told him about the way the sun felt on my arms that day and about the wind in my hair and how tan I was getting, I could feel it. The sun was on me, and we were laughing, all of us, Caroline and Rebecca and me, because we knew we looked better when we were tan, and what a relief it was that our mothers were going to let us lie in the sun that day.

You know how Mom is about the sun, I said, and I could feel Buck nodding into his pillow next to mine.

Well, anyway, I told him, *I was lying on my towel with the sun on my face, leaning back on my elbows and feeling myself getting red.*

All the mothers were after us about the sun, about premature aging and sunspots and skin cancer, because they're getting older, but I don't know why they all cared so much, because as far as I know, at least with our mother, Dad doesn't look at her skin, or at any other part of her. He's too busy playing his games in the living room every night with his Nerf ball. He's like a little kid with those basketball games, that's just how he is now, and there's nothing anyone can seem to do about it.

So there I was, I told Buck, *getting all this good color when the blue girl started to drown. I could barely see her from my towel since she was swimming all the way out past the buoys where no one was supposed to go, but who was going to stop her? She did what she wanted to do, because people were afraid of her, and they still are. In that way I guess she's lucky. No one bothers her.*

Anyway, the water was bubbling up out past the buoys, when Magda started screaming that there's a girl drowning out there, doesn't anyone see it?

She reminded me of all the summer mothers right then. Why didn't she get up off her ass and jump in the water herself if she was so goddamned concerned, and Buck always laughs each time I say *ass* and *goddamned* even though I'm careful to add that he shouldn't say those words, and that she's not like those fat-assed summer mothers, not really, even if she didn't get up that day.

Some of those summer mother are just fat asses, I said, and Buck laughed again, his sleepy laugh, and then I told him again not to curse.

Promise me you won't say fat ass, I said, and he said, *O.K., I promise I won't say fat ass,* and we both started laughing.

Buck was cute, curled up like that. And he's cute when he dances, even when he tells me his dreams, which are mostly annoying, except for the one about my dad getting trapped in a giant net. That one scares him.

Anyway, I told him, *Magda was standing there screaming, and I wanted to scream back at her, at all of them, to tell them all to stop looking at me and to run into the water and go get her themselves. I thought that was what mothers were supposed to do. I didn't think it was up to me. I was on my towel and then I wasn't, I was on my feet running toward the water, which was freezing, so cold I could barely feel myself breathe. The girl was way out there. I dived in headfirst and swam as fast as I could, my heart racing, my arms getting heavier with every stroke as I tried to get out there to get her. All I could see were her arms, blue as the night, coming out of the water and pounding back down again, and she was making all sorts of noises in her throat. Just as I reached her, my hair got caught in the cable between the buoy and its anchor. For a minute, she looked right at me and opened her mouth, but no scream came out, just a fistful of water. I was moving my arms as fast as they'd go, but they felt so heavy until I got my hair untangled from the buoy cable and managed to wrap my arms around her waist. She kept pounding the water with her fists, and she wound up punching me in the face.*

Did it hurt? Buck asked, yawning while scratching the sailboats on those crappy polyester pajamas Mom keeps buying him.

Did what hurt?

He stopped scratching and closed his eyes.

The blue girl, he said, *when she punched you.*

Yes, I told him, *of course it hurt, it hurt for a long time—remember the bruise I had? She didn't mean to punch me,* I explained, *she was fighting to live. That's what people do when they're drowning, when they feel their lungs being crushed inside their chests and the water burning in their throats. Yes, it hurt, but the pain wasn't enough to stop me, and once I had her and started dragging her in, she didn't feel heavy, she seemed to just float.*

Like she was dead? he whispered.

Yes, I said, *like she was dead.*

Dead man's float, he said.

Once I had her and she was floating along with me, I could see Mom crying at the edge of the shore through the water splashing in my eyes, and Magda, too, and Libby and Rebecca and Caroline, they were all crying when I flopped her down on the sand, on her back. Everyone was crying except me, me and the blue girl, because she wasn't breathing. Maybe right then, she was really dead.

I was about to tell him how I pressed my mouth down on hers and took in a huge breath, the biggest and longest breath I ever took, and for a minute I just held it in, all that air, kept it down inside my lungs and I was never going to let it go. I was about to tell him how huge I felt with that breath inside me, how everything expanded, not just my chest and lungs but everything: my blood, my nose, my hair, and all the things deep inside that I'll never see. I was about to tell him the best part, how when I breathed into her mouth I felt as if I just kept getting bigger, as if I could somehow keep expanding forever. But then I heard Buck's breath slowing, and I kept the rest of the story for another night—a night that might never come, because every time I've told him this story, he's always fallen asleep, and always at the best part.

Mom has been driving us to school lately. She always drops Buck off at grammar school first, and then winds through town the long way, past the woods, the woods that lead to where the blue girl lives. She never looks at me during that part of the drive, but I know what she's after. I know she wants me to talk about her. I know that's what she wants, but I know that if I stay quiet, then she won't ask.

This morning, when we get to school I hunker down in my seat watching the others file in, kids I've known all my life in this stupid town, kids whose mothers don't drive them in a station wagon and talk about the kind of nonsense that comes out of my mother's mouth. Although maybe I'm wrong, maybe they all talk the way she does, I don't know. I like to think other mothers are different, not like mine, staying up late, baking strange pies that she keeps in the refrigerator and says she's saving for a bake sale that never happens. You know, I've lived in this town my whole life, and I don't remember a single bake sale, not even for band uniforms or books for the school library.

Are you staying after school today? she asks as I gather up my backpack and unlatch the seatbelt that's been choking me the whole ride.

I shake my head, and she says, *Well, I just want to tell you that we're having chicken tonight with baby carrots and squash. You know that squash is your father's favorite.*

I don't know this. If anyone asked, I'd have to say that I couldn't name any of my father's favorite foods, or his favorite colors, or his favorite anything.

I thought Nerf balls were his favorite, I say over my shoulder as I close the door and walk away. *Maybe you should bake some Nerf balls. He might even eat them,* I add.

She opens her eyes wide when I say that, and looks at me as if she's about to reach over and slap me. Part of me wishes she would. Part of me wishes she'd hit me in the face, in the cheek, right here, right below my eye and next to my nose, right where the blue girl punched me.

But of course she goes home to de-bone her chicken and do whatever it is she does during the day. Tonight we'll sit at dinner, heads bent over her squash, listening to my father swallow. Maybe she'll bake more of the pies with the chocolate and the sugar and the things she thinks we don't see. They seem to make her feel better, those pies, and I don't want her to feel bad, I really don't. It's not my fault that she's the way she is, or that my father is afraid of the television, or that I was the only one who wasn't afraid to save a girl that everyone thought was dead. Or maybe it is.

In biology we're studying the epidermis and the three layers of skin that coat our bodies. Caroline and Rebecca and I sit at a table together so we can both copy Caroline's notes. I don't really need Caroline's notes, or at least I didn't used to, back when I still slept at night, and Rebecca tries to be dumb, because she thinks being both smart and pretty are too much. The guys in our grade all lean against their lockers and make a big show of watching Rebecca walk when we pass by, and Caroline and me, too, but only because we're with Rebecca. Most of the guys are still tan from the summer, but it's not an improvement, and the teacher,

Mr. Davis, makes Greg stand up and uses his freckles as an example of whatever it is he's trying to teach us.

We're all laughing at Greg because Greg's not even supposed to be in the class since he's a year ahead of us and because Greg is making faces at Mr. Davis when he isn't looking; Mr. Davis, who lives out of town and never gets any sun. I'm drawing circles in my notebook as big as Greg's freckles and lean over to watch Caroline writing "epidermal pigmentation" in big letters across the top of the page. I write it down too, because if I know one thing, and I don't really know all that much, I know that whatever Caroline writes has to be important.

Sometimes I want to ask her about my father's brain, because Caroline knows a lot about the brain. Once, at a sleepover at my house, she told me all kinds of things she knows about the brain, about the stem and the synapses, the things that make Ethan so slow because his are all broken. I wonder if my father's synapses are broken now, too. I reach over to write a note in Caroline's notebook when I feel my breath go cold in my throat. Cold. Like hers.

Mr. Davis calls on Caroline because he knows she's the only one worth calling on. I think he must feel sorry for Caroline having a brother in the same class, a brother who failed his class last year. He hardly ever calls on me or Rebecca, and if anyone has a brother they should feel sorry for, it's Rebecca, but she doesn't feel sorry for Ethan because to her, he's just her brother, not someone to be pitied. I understand that. I think about my dad, and I remember how I feel at night when I'm alone in bed and I smell my mother baking those pies in the kitchen and the smell of the marshmallow seeps under my door. I think of those nights when I see blue in the insides of my eyelids, when Buck doesn't come to tell me his dreams or ask me to tell my story one more time. And I admire Rebecca for not feeling sorry for her brother, but I can't help feeling just a little bit sorry for all of us.

What about the girl? Caroline asks Mr. Davis. *The one who lives out by the lake. The one who's supposed to be blue?*

Rebecca drops her pen on the floor, and I can hardly breathe. Everyone turns to look at Caroline, but she doesn't look away, she just keeps staring at Mr. Davis, who's gone whiter than any of us have ever seen him, white like someone who's about to pass out right then and there.

Rebecca grabs my hand under the table. *It's O.K.,* she mouths to me, but I know how not O.K. it is. My hands are cold, but Rebecca's fingers feel hot against them. Mr. Davis is saying something about the girl—that she's just a rumor, an idea, that girls with blue skin don't exist and certainly don't live in this town and that if we know what's best for all of us, we should study for the test. I look up at him for just a minute, and he looks away as I think of the water on my face and the feel of the girl's lips when I was breathing into her as hard as I could. I try to remember how it felt to take in that breath and hold it, and then give her that breath, and how good it felt, how big. That feeling is gone now, though, and I can't get it back no matter how hard I try.

Magda

TO WATCH A GIRL DROWN IS A TERRIBLE THING. TO watch her being revived is even worse. To watch a girl stay blue even after she breathes again, this is the worst thing I can imagine.

In all my years at the lake as a child, I never saw anyone drown; I never saw anyone fall into a deep pocket or even cough up swallowed water. In that lake I learned to swim, when the water still looked like glass. I taught my own children to swim in that lake when they were babies. *Don't be afraid,* I said, as they kicked their little legs. *It's only water.*

I go over that day when the girl started drowning, over and over it, and still I can't think why I didn't help. Why I didn't jump in, why I didn't swim out to her, why I didn't even try. I've never been afraid of water, never, not for even a minute. I knew I wouldn't drown. If there's one thing I've known all my life it's that I won't drown.

I used to be one of the summer people. Used to be, but no more. I stayed. Only a few of us stay, and I am one of them. I used to love this town when I was one of the summer people, but now it's just a summer getaway town that becomes dull when the summer people leave, like any other small town with a lake not too far from a big city. Except for the girl, who's made everything different, even the lake where I swam as a child.

My parents came from Russia and made money in textiles. They told me, *Magda, marry well, marry safe, forget happiness; there is no happiness in marriage.* Although their marriage had been arranged, they seemed happy enough endlessly playing durak, but when they took their children to the beach to watch them swim in the quiet lake, they hoped we would meet the children of privileged people. They said the kind of people who could summer in a cottage were the kind of people we should know. I remember sitting on my mother's lap while she rubbed lemon in my hair to bring out streaks, my brothers throwing stones into the lake to make ripples and how I liked to step into the largest ripple just before it broke apart. *If I could only stay inside that ripple,* I used to think, *anything would be possible.*

Eventually I found a way to stay. I met a townie boy with long hair and gangly limbs who made me laugh. We danced in those ripples out at that lake, and in those ripples I got myself pregnant. My parents wept. They said, *This boy will bring you no happiness, Magdalena,* and I said, *To hell with happiness, you said so yourself.* Mama said, *Said who?* And I said, *You did, Mama, you.*

Year after year, the town more grew increasingly dull. The summer people seemed to grow younger. The children grew. My parents died. My brothers said our parents had never seemed as happy as they had in their old age, playing durak and telling jokes in Russian. Meanwhile the townie boy became a man. He still keeps his hair long but no longer makes me laugh.

One day toward the end of summer, when the children were fighting, Greg and Caroline—Greg the Boy, who helped keep me here, and sensible Caroline, who reminds me of why I stay—I left the house and drove out to the lake to throw stones. They skimmed the water the way my brothers had taught me when we were summer people, embarrassed by our parents' English. When the ripples floated toward me, I went into the lake in my jeans and sandals and stood until the first big ripple broke through my body. Right after, the blue girl came from nowhere, and I thought, *Now I have to stay.*

In bed at night when I can see traces of the townie boy in my man-husband, I sing, *Tell me your secrets, I'll tell you no lies.* He smiles and says, *You used to sing to me all the time. Do you remember?* I smooth back the graying longish hair with my fingers, an old habit, and say, *No, I don't remember. What did I sing?*

Of course I remember, but there is such a thing as telling too much, Mama used to say. Some things you should keep inside. And so I do.

Greg the Boy swears in the house. When I named him Gregorio and nicknamed him Greg, Mama took him in her arms and said, *This boy will always be a boy, Magda, this Gregorio, this Greg the Boy.*

He has always been impetuous, this boy of mine, reluctant to take direction, even at three-and-a-half. Try to teach him to ride a tricycle, this boy knew better. But this swearing is new, *fucking this and fucking that,* and all of this grabbing he does. I don't remember my brothers having mouths like his or moving their hands the way this boy does, but I think Mama was right about him. *Greg the Boy.*

He comes into the house and throws his sneakers on the floor and says, *That fucking blue girl, man, she is so fucking blue, how the fuck does someone get so fucking blue?*

This is the son who kept me here, who grew inside me and became this swearing, freckled, lanky boy who can't keep his hands to himself. Such a boy this boy is, with *fuck* on his mouth. He wants a rise out of me, but I won't give it to him. Mama taught me too well how to play along.

I say, *Listen, boy, this is no way to talk in my fucking house, and there are other girls you should be worried about. Leave the blue girl alone.*

I can play his game.

He laughs and says, *Ma, you are such a fucking gas.*

He walks about the kitchen with his hands moving around in his pockets, his head slung low like it's too heavy to carry, like he hopes his head will snap off. I know the feeling. I am making the pies, baking the cookies for the tops and the bottoms, mixing in the chocolate, because we're meeting tonight, and I need to assemble all the parts of the pies. I had never heard of moon pies before this, before Irene said we should visit the girl and bake moon pies for her. She called this morning and said, *We need to go tonight, Magda, it's Tuesday, don't forget,* and I said, *Don't worry, we'll go, there is no way I can forget what day it is.*

Greg with his sloping shoulders and freckled hands thinks he can get away with standing in my kitchen while I make the pies, but I say, *Get out of my kitchen, boy, you are failing biology.*

He says, *How the fuck do you know?*

I say, *I have my fucking ways.*

I get out the bowl and mix the vanilla and the egg whites and the marshmallow cream into the filling. He's failed biology, this boy who kept me here, this boy who cannot understand cells when it was the splitting of cells that made me stay in this sorry town.

Zygote, I say, shooing him with my spoon.

He says, *What's that?* And I say, *You should know, my boy, you of all people should know, before you have one of your own.* He lumbers out with his hands at his sides, his arms like puppets with the hands broken.

After the filling is ready, I start melting the chocolate. This is the best part, the stirring of the chocolate as the bubbles rise up and then pop. I move my spoon around and around, stabbing at bubbles with the wooden handle. When I stir the chocolate, I imagine each dark brown bubble absorbing my secrets, one at a time.

Are they secrets or little white lies, I wonder, *and what is really the difference? Who's to know when you break them into small bites and watch them disappear down a girl's throat?* I watch the chocolate bubbling. Tiny bubbles, my life in a pot.

Tiny bubbles, I start to sing.

Caroline shuffles into the kitchen. Her hair is pinned back in barrettes, an unflattering zigzag part in her hair that all the girls are wearing now. But when she came down the stairs this morning, she leaned down to show me her scalp and the butterfly clasps that held her hair back from her forehead and asked me how I liked it, I thought, *Why make a fuss?*

Very much, I said.

Tiny bubbles, tiny bubbles. I don't know the rest of the words.

As she leans against the sink with her arms crossed over her chest, the butterflies look trapped. *Mama, you look so happy when you make your little pies,* she says.

I turn to her and toss her one of the broken cookie tops from the cooling rack on the counter. She's getting thick at the waist, the Russian blood coming out in her with her heavy hands and squat legs. If only Mama had lived to see her grow up.

I say, *Who said anything about making pies?*

The cookie disappears inside her mouth. I throw another and another piece to make her laugh. Anything to keep her from the pies.

Greg's failing biology again, she says.

The chocolate thickens. I stir and stir. The cookie pieces are setting on the cooling rack, not quite ready for their chocolate covering.

I know, I say.

What? she asks.

Nothing, I say. *Never mind. But I have my ways, you kids should know, I have my ways.*

Under the cabinet I find an oven mitt with faded sunflowers, part of a pair my mother bought me when I first got married. *To bake bread for that blond boy of yours,* she explained, but I've never baked bread for him, not once. I can cook, it's true, but I've never liked it. Moon pies are all I've been able to enjoy.

They are ready for the chocolate, the cookie tops and bottoms that make up the pie. I let out a little whoop inside myself so Caroline doesn't hear. She can't have a mother whooping about the kitchen, it will give her ideas. The girl's mouth appears inside my mind, open, with blue skin giving way to a pink tongue, like a cat's, except without ridges.

Are those for us? Caroline asks. *I'm hungry.*

I am ever the disappointing mother.

No, I say, and when she looks down at her sneakers and bends to tie the laces, I say, *I'm making something special for you. These are for the bake sale, too sweet anyway, no good, they'll rot those beautiful teeth.*

This much is true. If Caroline has one beautiful thing about her, it's her teeth. They shine. As a child, her baby teeth always glowed. At the lake the summer people would stop me as I paddled her in the water and ask, *How do you get your baby's teeth so white?*

I'd say, *Baking soda.*

They'd look at their own babies' teeth with the milky film across them and squint their eyes at me.

Something from the old country that I learned from my mother, I'd say.

I never touched her teeth. What she brushes with now, I have no idea, but it's not with baking soda, that much I'm sure of. What kind of mother would shove baking soda into her baby's mouth?

Caroline smiles when I mention her teeth and slides one of her barrettes off. Now, with just the one strand hanging loose, she looks so much softer, so much less severe, so much less like my mother.

Mr. Davis made Greg get in front of the class today. I was so embarrassed, she says. *And Audrey, I thought Audrey was going to cry when I asked why the girl out there is blue.*

The mitts feel tight around my hands. I set the tray on top of the oven to cool and think of Audrey sprinting toward the water, bone thin, pulling the girl out.

I tug at the oven mitts on my hands and look at her.

Why would you ask such a thing? I say.

Caroline says, *Because everyone wants to know. Everyone asks about the day she almost drowned.*

Steam rises from my cakes. When I smell something in the air, I rush back to the stove and lift the pot off to keep the chocolate from burning.

I ask, *And what did Mr. Davis say?*

Caroline looks at the moon pies that I won't allow her to eat. The filling is nowhere near as white as her teeth—even bright marshmallow filling can't compete with teeth like hers.

He said there was no such thing, Caroline says, and I smile at her and say, *Smart man.*

Greg comes back in and hovers over the stove. He has always been a hoverer, this boy, always lurking.

One of the cookies falls to the floor. My son—with his gangly arms and freckles the size of quarters, freckles no one in my family has ever had—picks up the broken cookie and takes a bite.

With a mouthful of cookie he says, *Fucking blue girl,* and I say back to him, *Now that is fucking enough.*

I call Irene to ask her what time we should meet, and as I'm dialing I think her name is the name of a song, maybe a song I used to sing. What were the words? *Irene, good-night Irene*—what was so special about Irene? *Something,* I think, *made the Irene in that song special,* but what it was, I can't remember. Maybe the visits to the blue girl are taking my memory. I don't know. I don't remember.

Irene, good-night Irene, I sing into the phone when she picks up. *What time, Irene?* I ask.

She whispers. I can hardly hear her.

What? I say.

Same as always, she says, and hangs up.

Irene's a nervous woman with a nervous daughter and a crazy husband, though I can't blame Audrey for being nervous after saving the girl that day. She's thinner than ever, and once I asked Irene, *Is she eating?* Irene said, *Of course she's eating, I cook for her every night.* It was the wrong question. I knew it as soon as it came out of my mouth. I have that way about me, like Mama did. She once asked a woman at a fruit stand if she shaved her legs above the knee.

So smooth, she said, *is why I asked.*

Mama, I told her, *some people don't like observations made about them, even if the observations are nice.* And she said, *What observation? I like things smooth.*

The nights we go to the woods, I miss my mother. Papa not as much, since he was quiet and let Mama do most of the talking, but Mama—I miss her humor, I miss the way she phrased things, even though they embarrassed me as a kid. I even miss her disappointment in me. I wonder what she'd say about this girl who lives in our town out in the woods with an old woman. *No family?* she'd say. *But you feed her. Feeding is good.*

Not even in my imagination do I let her ask me what I feed her.

David's on the couch watching television when it's time to go, belching up my stroganoff. *Tastes even better coming up,* he laughs. I sit on the couch beside him and think of the blond boy who swam after me in the lake and first slipped his fingers inside in a way that made my head fall forward against his chest like I might never be able to lift it again. David, I told myself, slayer of giants. A good name for a man to marry, regardless of the boy who grew inside me who actually made me marry him. Now he owns the kayak rental at the lake and serves the summer people, but that is what marriage will do.

I tell him I have to go. I have to meet the girls to deliver the pies for the bake sale.

Another bake sale? he asks.

You should know what kind of town this is, I say. *You grew up here, not me. It's not my fault we're in this fucking town.*

He lays a hand on his thigh and looks over at me in a way he hasn't looked in a long time.

He says, *Now you sound like Greg.*

It will pass, I say, and then I almost say, *The swearing doesn't really worry me. It's what he does that keeps me up at night.*

I tell him to check to make sure they've done their homework, especially biology, which he's failing again, and to please compliment Caroline on her hair. *She's very sensitive these days. We don't want her thickening any more than she already has.*

He leans into me close and says, *What happened to that wild girl who shook out her hair in the water? Who would have ever guessed you'd become such a fine, domesticated woman?*

My mother, I think, *that's who.*

People change, I say, as I look around the room at my needlepoint, the ceramic mugs the kids made in grammar school, the pictures of our wedding when we looked so young and stupid—and he says, *I guess they do.*

He asks me if I've left any of the pies for the kids in case they want a snack, and I tell him I've made them something different, something special, that I would never deprive my children. What kind of mother does he take me for?

Irene is waiting for me in her station wagon, the same car she's had for ten years. The doors are starting to rust. Everyone knows her husband is crazy, Colin, who never speaks, who throws a ball in the house like a child. I can count on one hand the number of things Colin has said to me over the years. He's not right in the head, that's true, but still, he could buy her a new car. There is family money, we've heard, though we do not ask. Now that he's crazy, he could part with some of that money for a car. At least that's what Libby and I say, but we don't ever tell Irene those things—we don't want to hurt her. Besides, if we talk about Colin, then we have to talk about Ethan, and none of us wants to do that, not even Libby, who keeps him in the house all the time except when he goes to school. It's no way to raise a boy, even one with such problems, but who am I to say? Talking about Colin makes Irene nervous, and she's nervous enough as it is.

I get out of the van and wave. She must not have seen me in the dark, because she doesn't even turn her head. I knock on the window, and her head snaps around so fast I can feel the burn up her neck from a crick like that. *She should slow down,* I think, as she opens the lock and lets me in.

She says, *The children are beginning to talk.*

I light the cigarette that I save for our nights that we go to the blue girl and crack my window. When I offer the pack to Irene, she takes one. Her hands are shaking.

I say, *It's just talk, Irene, it's just talk.*

Irene puffs on the cigarette, leans forward, and squints at the road ahead that leads to the house.

Buck dreams about her, she says. The smoke curls around her fingers. *He dreams about her every night.*

I blow smoke out the window. Mama loved to smoke when she was young. I imagine her sitting beside me, sucking on her unfiltered cigarette and laughing, saying, *Afraid of her own husband and children, this woman, such a shame,* and then clucking her tongue.

Irene, I say, *children talk. They dream. They do all sorts of things.*

She nods and stares at her cigarette.

Look at my boy, Greg, grabbing at Rebecca, I say. *They grow up, and they become strange.*

We don't say anything about Ethan, who is, of course, strangest of all, because such talk would be too sad, and there is too much sadness already. We sit and watch the road for Libby's car, always ten minutes late at least. Libby, with the beautiful daughter and the broken son. At night when I think of the blue girl, as I do every night, I think we all need these trips to see her, Libby most of all. But when I look at Irene with her shaking hands, I think I might be wrong.

She says, *Audrey doesn't sleep,* and I say, *I know. Caroline tells me. She has circles under her eyes, we've all seen them.*

And then I say, *Caroline asked about the girl at school, Irene. Asked the teacher. Maybe it's time you talked to Audrey. Maybe it's time we all talked.*

She glares at me, flinches as if I've poked her with a lit match, and says, *This is our secret. Ours. I thought we agreed.*

As the headlights of Libby's car beam straight at us, I cover my eyes with the back of my hand and touch Irene on the arm.

Then maybe you can talk about other things, I say.

She doesn't answer. The time for talking has passed. Libby walks over to us with her sweater draped over her shoulders, very stylish, wearing white slip-on shoes with her hair tied back. We kiss each other's cheeks and wait until Libby says the obvious.

What are we waiting for?

We laugh. Every time we visit the girl, we laugh. It's a laugh that almost hurts, not like the laughs we have when we talk about sex, like the time Irene told us that once, years ago, long before the television and the crazy basketball games, Colin fell off the bed in the middle of it, and she landed on top of him. Or when I told the story of David falling asleep while I went down on him with ice cubes in my mouth after too many shots of rum, although I'm kind of sorry I told that story, even though these are my friends, and who else can I tell? We laugh even though these stories aren't really funny—they make us look bad, they embarrass us, they show how unattractive we've become, even to our own husbands. Still, we have to tell each other more than just stories about the kids or cooking or summer gossip. We have to tell something about ourselves.

I'm the first to go in, always, but since the last time when the blue girl choked, I've been wanting to go last. But we have a routine, that's one thing we've always agreed on. It's a ritual, and we have to abide by it. I hear Mama whispering approval, Mama, who was so fond of order. The girl seemed peaceful in her bed that first time we visited, with her fingers interlocked and white blankets draped over her. Her breath came slow and deep and didn't whistle. She opened her mouth as soon as I unwrapped the moon pie. After she swallowed a bite, she smiled at me with rapture.

You like that? I asked. And when she nodded, I broke off a piece and gave her another. Each bite made me feel lighter. I felt bubbles in my head like after too much champagne.

I thought of every lie I'd ever told, and though there were too many to count, I felt hopeful. That first night, feeling as if I'd fed the blue girl all my lies, I swam nude in the lake before I went home. Although the ripples washed over me, I couldn't see them breaking in the darkness, I couldn't tell where the ripples ended and I began. It made me cry, swimming that way. I thought about David as the lanky boy I met that summer, the way we made love in the lake, the way I leaned my head against him as he sucked on my breast, the way he tugged at it with his teeth like he wanted to swallow me whole, and I wanted him to. I pressed my chest forward to give him more of me, but there was never enough to give.

During the last few visits, the girl looked restless. She sat up in bed and stared, not lying back like she used to, not opening her mouth until the moon pie was almost at her lips. At the last visit she choked, and I began to cry. I hadn't cried for so long that it hurt to stop. She swallowed one of the pies whole and opened her mouth to show me she couldn't breathe. When she tried to grab for my hand, I ran out to the room where the old woman waits and then out to my car, crying all the way.

If we can just hold on, it will be all right once it's over, Magda, Irene said when she joined me, and I said, *I know, but sometimes it's just so hard.*

Tonight the old woman is waiting by the door. She's small and hunched and keeps her hands hidden in her pockets. As her hands move inside the pockets, I imagine they're filled with nuts. *When we're gone,* I think, *she'll crack the nuts open with her teeth.* She motions to us, but it's so dark I can only make out the outline of her hand—I can't see what she's hiding. I think that if Mama were here, she could talk to the old woman—not in English, not in Russian—in some strange, unknown language, and she could get her to open her hands. But I don't have Mama's gifts.

The old woman says, *She is very hungry,* and gives me a look of such meanness, I almost crush the moon pies before I remember they're in my hands. She says, *You took so long to come, the girl is starving. The girl needs to be fed.*

Irene says she's sorry, but we have children who need us, things to attend to, we don't mean to be forgetful. The old woman doesn't answer. She pokes at my moon pie with her finger.

Go, she says, and I hurry through the small room with no chairs, almost tripping as I head down the hallway to her door. I think of knocking, but she's always in bed, this girl, so I turn the knob and go inside.

She looks bluer than before, but how this is possible, I don't know. How she became blue in the first place is a mystery to us all, how she breathes, where she came from, what she wants. What we want from her.

Standing here feels so much like a dream that I'm sure I'll wake up in a minute and find Mama shaking me in my bed, telling me it's time to go swimming in the lake, time to get some sun on my face. I think I'll wake up and there will be no husband who ignores me, no limp-haired daughter, no boy who worries me with his swearing. It will just be me and Mama and Papa playing durak. I'll be one of the summer people again. My brothers will throw rocks in the lake, and I'll dance in the ripples.

She's sitting up in the bed looking less serene than usual. There's no peace in her face, her brows knit together, her crazy hair juts out worse than Caroline's. I think of offering to comb her hair. I think the girl would like that, would like a mother's touch, except that I'm no good with hair.

I say, *I brought you pies, your favorite.* And when she smiles. I say, *I hear you're very hungry.*

It's the first time I've seen her nod. Her head moves slowly, up and down, up and down again, like a baby when you first teach it to say yes or no, even though no is always the favorite.

I ask if she'd like one of my pies, and she nods again, up and down, her whole neck bending then coming slowly up. It looks like a great effort, this nodding, but she smiles when she does it, so I think it must not really hurt. Her blue lips part as I hold out a piece for her. She closes her eyes, smiling while she chews, and I think of Mama saying, *This girl, so easy to please. You were that way once.*

When she finishes three pies in just a few big bites, I watch for signs of choking, but they seem to go down smoothly, no gasps. When she swallows the last bite I hear the song in my head, loud at first, *tiny bubbles,* then a soft *tiny bubbles . . .* I wish the girl knew the words.

I'm about to get up when she lets out a grunt, a low noise in her throat, so low it stops me, and I fall back in the chair.

I unfold the empty napkin as if to say, *That's it, no more,* but she shakes her head back and forth, childlike. She holds out her hand to mine. I don't take the hand. I just look at it. Even the fingernails are blue.

I say, *No more, that's all I have.* She shakes her head at me again. I get up from the chair and move toward the door. Libby's next, I think, and she can't wait with Ethan home, so there's no time for lingering.

When I'm halfway to the front door, the old woman says, *There is always more, so much more. You have no idea how much more.*

I don't look back. I move out the door as fast as I can. I don't even wait for Irene or Libby the way I'm supposed to. All I can think is that I have to get home before something happens, although I have no idea what that something might be.

I drive fast with my foot hard on the accelerator and my hands tight at the wheel. Mama sits in the passenger seat next to me, holding cards in her hands. She says, *So much pain that girl has. Why don't you take away the pain?*

I blink, and Mama's gone. In my head I tell her, *I'll make more moon pies, Mama, I promise I will.* But I am no good with promises, and she knows that.

Greg the Boy is up when I get home. For a minute I want to take him in my arms the way I did when he was small and his freckles were still cute. We used to play connect the dots on his arm. Now we'd need to draw a highway map.

He says, *Ma, where are all the fucking pies?*

I stand there looking at this boy, this son of mine, who pulls at his groin and fails biology. I think someday when I'm gone he'll imagine me in his car with him, and he'll think about the smell of my pies. I wonder if that's all he'll remember, his mother who made moon pies. That can't be all. There must be more.

He rattles around in the refrigerator. It's late, and I'm so tired.

Again he says, *Who took all the fucking pies?*

I stand there in the kitchen, looking at this boy of mine. If I close my eyes, I can hear the girl's breath whistling behind me when I ran out to the car. It was like a song.

I say, *Never mind the pies, it's time for you to go to bed.*

For once the boy listens. He ambles out in that way he has, head hanging low, his feet seeming to float.

Alone in the kitchen, I whisper that I'm the one who took the pies. The pies are mine. And there will be more.

Caroline

Epidermis.

Pigment.

Melanin.

Every time Mr. Davis teaches something new, I can't think about the words on the next test, all I can think about are cells. If I could cut my body open like a frog, I wonder how many cells would be inside. I wonder if I could count them all, and if I could, how long it would take. I imagine it would take my whole life, that I could probably spend all my remaining days counting and never finish. It would be a goal though, something to strive for, and I need goals, that much I know. Maybe if I spent all my time counting my cells, I wouldn't be thinking of Ethan's brain filled with all those mixed-up synapses, or Greg's brain filled with endorphins. Instead I could think about the difference between voluntary and involuntary impulses, and what would happen if the involuntary part of my brain just stopped firing neurons. I'd stop breathing, like the blue girl at the lake. I'm not even sure I really saw her anymore. Was she really blue, or did my brain etch a picture into my memory, making me think I saw her? Really, what guarantee do we have that we're going to keep breathing from minute to minute? How do any of us know whether at any second—like right here, right now—we won't just stop?

My obsession with my brain has gotten worse. Every night, and sometimes during the day, especially during biology, I keep thinking about my brain. When Mama talked to me over her pies, I'd wonder if she knew I was thinking about my brain instead of listening to her. I did try to listen as she talked about her mother, my grandmother from Russia, and sometimes I'd think about asking for a taste of the chocolate or the vanilla-scented filling, but then I'd start thinking about my brain sending its hunger messages to my stomach, and I would will it to stop. I imagined my thoughts swimming along the convolutions. I thought I could feel my neurons firing like gunshots.

At night in bed, I keep thinking, *What if something happened to my basal ganglia? What if my cerebellum stopped functioning? What if the neurotransmitters dried up? What if the pathway between my spinal cord and cerebral cortex got clogged? And what if my gray matter turned blue?*

I think about my heart and my lungs all the time. It's all tied into my brain, which I have no control over, and sometimes when I sit in Mr. Davis's class, I keep thinking that my brain has turned against me.

It says on the web that we're only born with a certain amount of gray matter and no more. It's finite. I don't think Greg has much gray matter at all, since he doesn't even understand biology. Rebecca has more than Greg, but I don't think she has as much as Audrey. I think Audrey has the most. Much more than I do. When Audrey pulled the girl out of the lake, I stood there with my eyes closed just like everyone else. Audrey is the one who knows what to do.

What if Audrey's gray matter turned blue when she saved her?

Not long after she saved the girl, I slept at Audrey's house. I hadn't slept there since her father got taken away, and Mama thought maybe it wasn't such a good idea, sleeping there with Audrey's dad not long out of the hospital. But she relented because Audrey's mom needed us to stay with Buck. She didn't say why, but the three mothers were going out. That was the first night I smelled the vanilla and chocolate in the air at Audrey's house, the same smell that floats through mine, but I didn't mention it to Audrey, because she looked so tired. I think our moms were putting something over on us.

We were sitting in the den with the television off, Audrey and her little brother, Buck, and I, drinking Cokes. Buck was supposed to be in bed, but Audrey always lets him stay up. Her father played that weird basketball game of his in the living room. We watched him for a while, and I even clapped once when he scored a basket. He smiled at me, a half-smile out of the side of his mouth. I almost missed it. Buck and Audrey stared at me when he smiled, and I felt the way I do when my brain seems to turn against me and I go all red in front of other people. I tried to distract her by asking where her mom was, where she'd gone with Mama and Libby.

Audrey said, *She thinks it's a secret.* She laughed when she said that. I laughed, too, but I don't know why I laughed. I didn't get the joke.

Buck said, *Watch this, Caroline, this is about her,* and then he held his breath until his face started to go red and then blue. He fell on the rug. Audrey's father didn't even look at him, he just kept shooting the Nerf ball. Audrey had to jump off the couch and make Buck sit still until he caught his breath again.

That's enough about her, she said. She said it in a gentle way, though, not angry as I would have been if Greg had done something like that in front of my friends, holding his breath and falling down. It's bad enough Greg keeps pawing at one of my best friends and keeps going on and on about the blue girl. After it looked as if he'd settled down, Audrey walked Buck to his bedroom. I leaned over on my chair to hear.

Tell me again, he said, *tell me about her again.*

Audrey leaned down and said, *Not tonight, Bucky, go to bed now.*

I almost got up and went over to them. I wanted to whisper, *Yes, please, Audrey, tell it again. Tell us about how you saved her, Audrey. Did you feel it, all that blue skin and body? Do you think it got inside you?* because Audrey's so skinny now, with blue veins under her eyes. Audrey doesn't seem to worry if her brain might turn blue, not like I do.

Even though Audrey saved a girl who was almost dead, she doesn't think the things that I do, about whether she's turning blue inside, or whether she'll stop breathing. I didn't even see much of what happened, since I had my eyes closed most of the time, holding on to Mama, but now I'm the one who worries about dying.

The night of that sleepover, Audrey didn't sleep. I woke up almost every hour and heard her father shuffling around the living room playing his game. At about three or four in the morning, I got up to go to the bathroom and saw him sitting on the floor with the ball between his knees.

Doesn't it ever stop? I asked when I got back to Audrey's bedroom. I was on the floor in my sleeping bag, and Audrey was in bed with the palms of her hands pressed against her eyes.

No, she said. *It never stops.*

I should have said something then, anything. Audrey's become so pale and thin lately. That night she looked compressed somehow. Can someone's body compress itself? She yawns all the time and nods off during tests. I let her cheat all the time. It's the least I can do. I may have issues with my brain and worry about it all the time, but at least I don't have to live with the memory of saving the blue girl.

I have to study for the biology test so I won't fail like my brother, Greg. Mr. Davis says if you understand the cell, you understand the universe, but I don't think that's true, because no one understands the blue girl. Not even Mr. Davis. He doesn't even think she exists.

I try to understand my cells. At my desk I lift my arm up to the light and imagine them flaking off or circling together trying to build more skin. It makes me feel better to think about my skin regenerating itself, growing, working to keep me alive.

If I can stop thinking about my cells long enough, maybe I can figure out why the girl is blue. Rebecca wants to know. Greg wants to know. No one says, *I want to know,* but

I can tell. I can see the wanting in their eyes. Audrey wants to know more than any of us, even though she won't say so. I want to know, but I think Audrey's desperate to know most of all.

It's embarrassing to have an older brother in the same class. Greg doesn't seem to care, even though everyone thinks he's obnoxious and slightly stupid, but in a cool way, as if being an idiot is cool. They want to be like him, and I can see Rebecca staring at his crotch sometimes. I wish she wouldn't look at him that way. It makes me think of all the arousal her sympathetic nervous system is going through. I would rather not think about anyone's sympathetic nervous system or its arousal, but I can't help it. Rebecca's been different since the summer, since her boobs grew and she started sweeping her hair to one side.

Extracellular matrix.

Vacuole.

Bacteriophage.

I cannot make the words penetrate my brain. The words are like dead cells that won't regenerate. Last year, before the blue girl came and almost drowned, I was acing earth science. I got a 97 on the final exam. Mrs. Gordon, the teacher, wrote, *Bravo, Caroline!!!* with three exclamation points. I used to be able to read the glossary in the back of the book and memorize all the terms in one try. When Mr. Davis made us map out gene combinations, I got up and filled in all the dominant and recessive genes without even studying.

I wonder if there's a recessive gene for blue pigment in the skin.

When Mama goes out, I stay on the computer all night. She doesn't like me spending that much time on the computer. She says it will ruin my eyesight and give me wrinkles in my forehead from squinting. She doesn't say it, but I know she thinks I don't need one more thing working against me when my waist is already rolling over on itself and my thighs are too thick. This morning I put pins in my hair to keep it off my face, and when I asked Mama how it looked, her face told me everything. *It looks nice, Caroline, very nice,* she said, but I knew it wasn't true. Mama's a very bad liar.

On the web I look up `"epidermal pigmentation."` It says, `"Sorry, no matches found."` I take one of the butterflies out of my hair and think about how many skin cells I might've killed just from sliding the pin against my scalp. It almost makes my cry. I type in `"blue" and "skin."` It says, `"The word 'and' is very common. Try another word."` My neurons feel like they're on fire. I type `"blue skin"` and up come all these hits. I remember Mr. Davis talking about random selection, so I close my eyes. I hold my finger out to see where it lands on the screen.

It's a questionnaire. I hear Greg thumping around downstairs, looking to steal Mama's pies. They smell so good, a sweet, creamy goodness that seeps right into the fat cells. Mama is right about that much. *They're for a bake sale,* she says whenever we ask her, and to me, Greg says, *When has there even been a bake sale in this fucking town?* And I say, *Shut up, Greg, those are Mama's pies.* He wants them, but he knows better. Mama loves those pies.

It takes ten minutes to download the questionnaire because my computer's so slow. Last week I asked Dad if he would think about getting me a new computer if I get an A in biology. He just looked at Mama and shook his head, and when we were alone, Mama said, *Don't ever look to a man for happiness, Caroline.* I told her I wouldn't, but I still want the computer.

The list is long. I print out the most important questions on page one:

```
Are the nail beds blue?
Does the person exhibit signs of
pulmonary edema?
Does the person have a persistent cough?
Is the skin blue at any points other than
arms, hands, and extremities?
```

I don't know what `pulmonary edema` is, but fortunately it's in blue and underlined, indicating a link. I click on it, and the new screen explains that it's a `"swelling of the lungs or lung tissue."`

That day at the lake, the girl didn't breathe for a long, long time. It seemed like forever when Audrey leaned over her and tilted her neck back exactly the way they taught us CPR at the end of last year on the dummy named Annie. Greg got in all that trouble for squeezing it and trying to mount it and for being a general pig. I sat next to Audrey in the gym that day, and I remember I couldn't pay attention because I kept thinking about my lungs and my own cilia and bronchial tubes. Everything could shut down at any minute. Nobody can prove that it won't. One second you could be breathing and the next your lungs could collapse. I didn't think Audrey was listening because she sat there looking down at the floor. I thought of asking her if she ever wondered how it would feel to have asthma or to just quit breathing, or if she felt her breathing was safe, but I knew how crazy it would sound so I didn't ask.

I guess Audrey listened better than any of us, because she knew just what to do that day. She turned the girl over just the way the woman had shown us that day with the dummy in the gym, and she used the flat of her hand when she pounded the water out of the blue girl's lungs. I can still remember the water spurting out, brown and thick with stench. When she pumped the girl's chest, I could see Audrey's mouth moving as she counted. She tilted the girl's head back. Everyone was yelling and crying: Rebecca's mother, even Mama. I looked up at Mama's eyes full of tears just when the girl started coughing.

Mama, I said on the way home, *don't be sad. Audrey saved her.*

Mama said, *Someday when you get older, you'll see that sometimes you wish you weren't someone's mama. You'll wish it was just you, you all alone.*

I didn't say anything, but I wanted to tell her that I felt that way already, even though I'm only fifteen. How will I feel when I get older and my cells start to die off and my gray matter gets soft? What will happen to me then?

When I hear Mama come in after midnight, I shut off the computer and climb into bed with the questionnaire under the blanket. It's dark, but I've already memorized the questions. `Cyanosis,` it said on the website. `Caused by lack of oxygen.` I breathe as deeply as I can and try to imagine the oxygen seeping into my cells.

I dream the blue girl is back. She's sitting outside on the grass behind the auditorium eating something out of aluminum foil. Rebecca and I stand by the window on the second floor looking down at her. She looks right back up at us. Her mouth moves very slowly as she eats.

She got bluer, Rebecca says.

Audrey comes up behind us. I turn around to her, but she looks right past me out the window. She's wearing a gray sweater that hangs off her shoulders. It looks like her shoulder bones might pop right out of her skin, and her eyes look all hollow with dark veins around them. I look down at her fingernails to check to see if they're blue, and they are. My poor friend Audrey, just a mass of cells.

Doesn't she look bluer to you? Rebecca asks.

I'm not sure if she's talking to me or to Audrey, so I don't say anything and neither does Audrey. We just stand there at the big window that looks out over the field and watch her as she picks stuff out of aluminum foil and eats it.

What do you think she's eating? Rebecca asks.

I think maybe cheese or pieces of meat, something with a lot of protein and vitamin B. She needs riboflavin to oxygenate her blood. Rebecca thinks she eats plants that grow out by the lake.

Maybe she eats blueberries, Rebecca says, and then she moves away from the window and says, *I'm going to find out.*

She turns around and walks down the stairs to the double doors that lead out to the field. I grab Audrey's sleeve to pull her along. Her feet shuffle when she walks, and for a second on the way down the stairs, I think that if I let go of Audrey, she'll fall and her bones will crack open as her body slams into the steps, and I won't know what to do because I haven't studied the skeletal system enough.

I reach over to hold both hands around Audrey's arm when Greg sneaks up behind us.

What the fuck do you think you're doing? Greg says.

Audrey slips away from me. Rebecca starts pulling on the door handle. The doors are made of metal, and they bang every time Rebecca yanks at the handle.

The blue girl's out there, I tell Greg.

No fucking way, Greg says.

Out of the corner of my eye I see Audrey leaning against the wall, shaking her head. I'm about to ask her what's wrong when the bell rings. I press my biology book hard against my chest and tell myself to think about my cells because it's getting harder and harder to breathe. I think, *Swollen epiglottis, bronchial obstruction,* when the door flings open, slamming against the wall and sending Rebecca flying into me. My biology book sails out of my arms and lands with a crack on the floor. The blue girl just stands there at the top of the stairs. Her lips tremble as she stands there staring at us. She looks at Audrey and then at Rebecca and then at me. I try to smile at her, but I can't, my lips won't move.

All of a sudden her mouth opens. She looks like she's going to speak, and then a wind comes out of nowhere, a huge gust that makes all the butterfly clips fly out of my hair. The wind blows harder. The glass rattles in the windows. I see Audrey in the corner, pinned against the wall by the wind, and I think, *Someone has to come, someone has to help us.* The blue girl's mouth opens wider, and the wind spins all around us. It hurts my ears. It sounds like screaming.

Greg yells, *Shut the fucking door!* but before anyone can move, the blue girl gets caught in the wind. It looks like slow motion, like a movie, her arms and hands twirling around in the wind. Her legs fly up in the air and her hair whips around. The wind knocks me down, hard. I feel the hard floor against my spine. A pain shoots through my lower back, and as I try to get up, I think, *I've broken a vertebra before I could memorize which one is which.*

Everyone runs out of the classrooms and into the hall. I lie on the floor with a stabbing pain in my back. Mr. Davis yells for everyone to crouch down and hold their arms over their heads like a crash position. Rebecca is screaming, Greg is screaming, *Fuck this! Fuck this!* The wind howls and blasts through the hall. I feel my body twisting as the wind blows me across the floor. Audrey reaches for my hand. *Hold on, hold on,* she says, and I grip her hand as hard as I can, so hard I can feel the ligaments in my arm stretching.

I lift my head for a minute. Every nerve ending in my brain must be shooting messages at once. My brain feels overloaded, but I keep my head up as long as I can to watch the blue girl spinning in the wind, to see if I can tell if she's breathing. When the wind finally stops, the girl stops in mid-air and then spits out a fountain of water that covers everything. All I hear, just before I wake up, is the splash.

Libby

I AM NOT A PERSON WHO DREAMS. SOME PEOPLE MIGHT say that this is not possible, that everyone dreams, that dreaming is part of the brain's natural function, that the psyche has to release, has to relieve itself, has to figure itself out. But for me, there is nothing to figure out. Diseases spread. We pass afflictions on to our children more terrible than anyone could imagine. We try to undo the undoable. Babies are born blue. People seem to die and then seem to live again, even though life seems impossible.

I used to dream but not anymore, not for a long time. When I did dream, I was a frequent dreamer. I kept a diary next to my bed and wrote the dreams down when I woke up. Before Ethan and Rebecca, I'd sometimes read the dreams aloud to Jeff in bed in the morning. He was never interested, I know that now. I complicated things, he told me years later, and he did what he could to settle me. Once he bought me a dream dictionary so I could look up the meaning of the symbols, but after Ethan was born it all stopped. I'd dreamed too much, Jeff said. It was time to wake up.

Now I am awake, or as awake as it is possible to be. I cannot imagine being more awake than I am now.

I haven't told the others, Magda and poor Irene, but when the blue girl first appeared that day on the lake, I felt awake for the first time in years. She was a rumor until then, a whisper overheard in the parking lot of the grocery store. A dream, except I'd stopped believing in dreams. When I heard about this strange blue person who lurked somewhere around the lake area—I don't think we knew then that she was a girl—I thought maybe I would be able to dream again, that I would look forward again to nighttime, to sleep. I felt comforted by the possibility of dreaming again. I thought there would finally be an end to this blankness. And there has been, even without new dreams, because I have awakened. The blue girl, who came to our woods and almost drowned in our lake, has awakened me.

Of course when I first heard about her I thought of Ethan. How could I not? I thought of the day he was born, how the doctor had told me first to push and then suddenly not to push so hard. My first baby—how was I to know how hard to push? Wasn't that the point, the pushing? Afterwards, they told me I'd pushed too well, that I was too good a pusher. He descended so fast, they said, faster than they'd wanted him to.

Why are they saying that to me? I asked Jeff.

He didn't answer. I kept waiting and waiting for them to bring the baby over to me, to lay him on my chest the way I'd seen in all the movies. They were cleaning him, the nurse said. I told her they didn't need to. Jeff told me to stop yelling, and I thought, *Who's yelling? Not me,* but I know now I must have been. The nurses gave each other looks. If I close my eyes, I can still see those looks. I'd like to ask them how they think it must have felt for a new mother, a first-time mother, lying there on the bed, not able to see her newborn son, wondering what those looks were all about. When we took him home, my mother told me that I could always have another child, that I could try again. *Try again at what?* I wanted to say, though of course I never said those words aloud.

When they finally handed him to me, I saw. I don't remember whether Jeff stood by my side or leaned over to me to look at the baby—his baby, just as much as mine—or whether he touched my hand or arm or kissed my forehead. I'd had all sorts of images of the birth in my mind before it happened. Yes, I anticipated the pain, but then I imagined the tears, the happy tears of witnessing the coming of a new life. There was none of that. When I held my son in my arms, I immediately saw that his head was large, his eyes close together, his face and hands a purplish blue.

He came down the canal so quickly, the doctor said, *that his color isn't quite right yet. He'll redden soon, not to worry.*

And his head? I said.

Jeff said nothing. Jeff did not look.

Possible encephalitis, he said. *We'll watch him. There will be a few tests.* And, *It could be nothing.*

The doctor reached out to shake Jeff's hand, and I remember that Jeff did not take it.

Now here we are in this town with a girl who almost drowned and then came to life again, living in a permanent state of blue. We didn't know what was wrong with her—we still don't—and yet I can't help but feel relief, knowing there is someone stranger than my son living out there in the world. Finally, there is something worse than a son with a mutated gene—fragile x syndrome, they call it—who bangs himself against the door at night, and speaks in a cartoon-like voice he has made up for himself. There is something worse than knowing you have killed off your own son's chances of normality without even knowing you could. And you can't undo it, you and your mutated gene on your x chromosome. Your daughter has been spared, but your broken son in this small town, he is a spectacle. Yet now, now there is someone else to wonder about at night across the black water, through the trees. Even the people who still think she's a dream, a game, a rumor to keep us all from being too bored, even they now wonder about her, instead of my son.

When I wake up this morning after our visit last night, the house still smells of the pies. I'm late getting the kids ready, and Jeff is already gone, as he always is, the only trace of him a splash of water on the counter and the stubble on his razor. And as usual, his side of the bed is made up, the covers tucked in. For years he has been trying not to leave even a trace of himself behind. In the early years he traveled as a salesman for a computer company, but the technology changed faster than he could, and now he sells electronics for a chain store in a town not far from here. It is my fault we stay in this town, even though we both grew up here, the fault has always been mine. He slips out of the house in the morning and into the bed at night without a coffee ground in the sink or a crease in the bedspread. Sometimes at night when he's lying there in his silent sleep, I lean over and whisper, *I know you're in there. I know you're really there.*

But now he's gone and Rebecca has made Ethan a bowl of cereal and turned on the little television in the breakfast nook so that he can watch cartoons and imitate the voices. Sometimes I look at them sitting there, my daughter with her perfect skin and hair like glass and my son with his finger motions—stimming, they call it—and strange sounds coming out of his throat, and I want to cry, right then and there, to put my head down on the counter and not raise it again until someone pulls me up and out of the chair, bodily picks me up, forcefully even, and shoves me back into my life. But then I smell the vanilla and the sweetness, and I know that she's out there waiting for me, for us, and that again we'll go and feed her, feed her our pain and our secrets along with the moon pies, and she'll take it all in and take it all away.

I lean over the table and kiss Rebecca on the top of the head—even her scalp shines—and I say, *Thank God for you, Rebecca, thank God.*

She looks over at her brother with his face pressed up against the tiny television and wipes a crumb away from her mouth.

Thank God for what, Mom? she says, and then, under her breath, she mutters, *Jesus.*

Just thank God, is all, I say. *That's it. Just thank God. Can't anyone thank God anymore?*

Ethan throws his head back and laughs a teeth-chattering laugh, and Rebecca says, *Not in this house.*

She smiles at Ethan, but when she gets up to rinse her plate, she says, *Speaking of God, the goddamned house stinks of vanilla.*

I say, *You're spending too much time with Greg.*

She doesn't deny it. She likes him. I've seen the looks, the sideways glances, the brushing up against her. I remember how it was. I was young and pretty—but not as pretty as Rebecca. All summer I watched my daughter become prettier until one day, it seemed, she moved from pretty to beautiful. I was pretty as a girl, but not beautiful, not like my own mother. Never beautiful. Sometimes I find myself wishing Rebecca were less beautiful. I think how happy my mother would be to see Rebecca now, how my mother always hoped I'd be beautiful. *There is always something to strive for,* my mother would say as she applied mascara and lipstick. *Anyone can be better.* It might be easier for Rebecca, though, if she were simply pretty. She'd have less to lose, fewer dreams to hold on to. Maybe she'll be lucky enough to remain beautiful, unlike pretty people like me, faded, without dreams.

I move to take Ethan's cereal bowl from him—always from the right side, never the left—and I am trying to take all three at once—bowl, napkin, and spoon—because the disruption of order is more than he can bear. Rebecca sees what I'm about to do and slides the spoon under my hand. She understands her brother in ways even I can't, in ways that Jeff has never tried to, and although I'm grateful for her—which is why I kiss her and thank God—there are times I can't stop myself from falling into the deep pit of "what if" . . . *what if* she has been damaged too, *what if* her understanding of her brother stems from having a recessive gene of her own—a permutation, they call it. *What if* she has early ovarian failure or her menopause comes on too soon. *What if* something were to happen to me or to Jeff, and Rebecca were left to take care of her brother? I take a deep breath and try to push these thoughts away while tipping the spoon into the bowl, waiting for the gap after the commercial to slide the bowl, spoon, and cereal away all at once.

This is when my mistake happens, when I drop the bowl. Because of all the dreaming I haven't been doing, I've fallen into a daydream of generations of chromosomal damage, of a daughter who may never bear children. And that's when the white ceramic bowl falls to the white ceramic tile floor, splashing white milk that clings to the silver spoon. It is like slow motion—milk, bowl, spoon, tile, crack—and I am staring at all the whiteness, at my son with his mouth open, screaming.

The chair falls back—also white like everything in my kitchen—as Ethan stumbles into me and begins banging with his fists and then with his head against the tile floor. Crack, crack, thud, crack.

The sound kills me, as it always does.

He yells again in his real voice now, the cartoon voice receding for the moment. Only when he screams and bangs and bangs and screams do I ever hear my son's real voice, deep-throated and heavy. It's the voice I used to hear in my dreams, back in that time when I used to dream of a teenage boy without an elongated palate and a too-long face that this fragile x has embedded into him. In my dreams, the teenage boy would stand in our white kitchen and smile with eyes that were never heavy lidded and blank, eyes that saw me, really saw me, not just the form of the mother who takes him for evaluations and keeps him out of group homes. The doctors say it could be my x or it could be Jeff's, there is no way to know. But I know that the x is mine. I know that I have done it. I know I'm the one who ruined him.

He cries now, following his own routine, the screaming giving way to this slower, deeper sound, the sound of my real boy stuck inside there, the blue trying to emerge in all this whiteness.

Rebecca slides herself across the floor in her too-tight jeans and grips him from behind, spooning against his back the way they taught us. Her hands grip his and pull them around his sides. How a girl so slim can be so strong I do not understand. And I don't understand how he never bruises Rebecca the way he does me. My arms are lined with bruises from the tantrums set off by dishes dropping or car alarms going off or too-loud toilets that flush down the hall.

Ethan, Ethan, Ethan, she says into his neck, and as he slows, she says it a fourth time because, somehow, fours speak to him. *Ethan.*

Her glassy hair fans out behind her. The two of them lie that way for a minute on the floor, neither of them moving. I think, looking down at them, of her, of the girl out on the lake that day, and then her lying on the sand with Audrey above her. I can almost smell the lake water coming up out of her throat, and I imagine my children are fish on the white floor. At least they are not blue. At least there is that. *If we could just stay this way,* I think, listening to their breath, the two of them safe and quiet on the floor, *maybe I'd never have to dream again.*

Mom, Rebecca says. *Help me get him up.*

I move to his left and hold my hands in front of him so he can see them before they startle him. Even my own bare hands are jarring to my son. When he goes to school on his little yellow bus, sometimes I drive out of town to a strip mall where I have my fingernails and toenails painted a stark red. Sometimes, on the way back to pick him up, I drive by the lake, and I park and just sit in my car, letting my hands hang out the window to dry in the sun. Then I get out, sit on a curb, and scrub all of it away with nail polish remover and cotton balls. Once I told Magda what I do, and she said, *Why would you do that, go to such trouble, only to have to take it off again?* I couldn't explain that I do it for my mother, wherever she is, to show her that I have not given up trying.

I manage to get him on the bus to his school in another district just outside of town where there are programs for boys like my son. Some of the others have Down syndrome and wave to me with their thick hands and almond eyes that disappear into their faces when they smile. The matron takes Ethan's hands in hers and leads him up the steps into the same type of bus he's been on since pre-school. Rebecca has gone inside to put on her mascara and lip gloss and to look at her reflection—to look at her shiny hair, her long lashes, and maybe, I think, if she could see it, her luck.

Say good-bye to Mama, Ethan, the matron says. Her name is Shelley, overworked Shelley, who has been hit in the eye and who sometimes has to bribe my son onto the bus with M&M's. Today, thankfully, there are no struggles. She winks at me once his seatbelt is fastened.

There you go now, Ethan, she says. *Ethan's O.K.*

He looks out the window, toward me but not at me, and says what has become his mantra of comfort.

Ethan's O.K., he says. He says it four times. *Ethan's O.K. now.*

When the bus pulls away, I stand in the driveway watching it become smaller and smaller and think about how I wish that was true, that Ethan was O.K.

Now it's night, and following my own routine, I lock Ethan into his room, wishing it could be otherwise. I started locking him in as a last resort after the alarms we installed failed, and I awoke too many times to find him up and wandering. I lie on the white bed with no discernable trace of Jeff. Sometimes he doesn't come home until well after midnight when the store has warehouse inventory. Or so he claims. I hardly ask anymore what his reasons are. If he's going to do it—erase himself—then why doesn't he just get it over with?

I hear Rebecca sliding open the glass door to the deck so slowly, so carefully, it makes me wonder how many times she's done it. I hear her feet on the driveway, and I know she's headed for the lake, for Greg. I think of getting up, of following her. I think of telling her not to do it. But I don't. I lie on the bed and think of my son sleeping in the next room with his mouth open, quiet, not banging. I know that soon we will drive to the lake in our separate cars, Irene and Magda and I, and we'll wonder whether we can ever step inside her blueness. I think of my daughter sneaking out to the woods with a boy, and I do not move. I do not stop her, and I do not dream.

Rebecca

GREG IS THE ONE WHO GETS US TO GO. HE'S BEEN saying it every day since school started, how he's going to go out there in the woods and find her and how he's going to get a look at her for himself. It's November now, the leaves are changing, and I'm tired. I just keep quiet and look at my hands when he talks and talks and talks. I wonder if Greg will talk so much when he's older, or if something happens to guys along the way that stops them from talking. Then they try to act like they're not there at all, like my dad, or they seem to go backwards, like Audrey's dad. I don't know much about Greg's dad, but he never says much to me either, and Greg does enough talking for both of them. There's nothing anybody can do about it.

Then there are boys like my brother who hardly talk at all.

Even Greg. Greg with the way he comes up behind me outside on the steps and swirls his tongue in my ear, soft and hot. It's not that I haven't liked it. It's not that I haven't let him do it, his tongue moving around and around, his hands up my sweater and all around. I sweat thinking about it. I've even let him move his hand inside me out in the backyard along the trees. But he's still a boy. I look at him and think: *A boy. A boy is what you are, and you don't even know it.*

We're out behind the annex at school when he really gets on about the blue girl and finding her. All of us going out to the woods. At first it's just him talking, talking, and talking the way he does. It's me and Caroline and Audrey and Greg, just the way it's always been since we were little, only Ethan used to be with us then, too, before they put him on the bus for the special kids, the little one that drives them all out of town. We'd all go out to the lake, all of us kids with our mothers, and run around with the kids who came only in summer. In pictures we look like any other little kids with tans. But then Ethan started talking in that voice of his and throwing blocks at school and biting the other kids. I saw the blue mark of a bruise on a teacher's arm once, and my mom wore long sleeves to hide hers. He's never bitten me, not then, not now. Once he bit my mom, a long time ago, and when she yelled for me to get him to stop, I held his head with the side of one hand and rubbed his jaw with the other to get him to release.

Like a dog, really, is how it was. There's no way to describe it, that feeling that your brother is like a dog, but that's what it felt like. Like he was a biting, foaming dog. Now he just bangs against his door at night, trying over and over to get out.

But Greg. Greg was different. Ethan never bit Greg, either. And Greg always talked to Ethan, even though Ethan never answered. I used to like Greg so much for that, like Ethan must have seen something kind in Greg. Even now, Greg will go on talking to Ethan, and Ethan just says things in that voice of his like he hasn't heard a word Greg has said. The rest of them are all the same, these boys I used to think I knew, all of them looking at me like I don't know what they want. When Greg does it, I close my eyes and think about the day the blue girl was drowning, the day Audrey saved her. I see her in my mind, dead on the beach, and then walking away, alive. I go to see her in my mind all the time, at night when Mom gets into her car and drives away, at night when I watch Ethan sleep in his white room. I go to the blue girl because I think maybe she can make it all stop.

And that, I guess, is why I've agreed to try to find her.

That fucking blue girl is what Greg calls her.

We just sit here. We look up at the trees and think about the girl. Lots of people don't believe she's real. I know they don't. Caroline and Audrey and I sit on the stone steps outside the annex, all of us just sitting around. Sometimes I think that all we ever do is sit and sit and wait and wait. Wait for the next laugh, the next day. Me, I wait for the next time we take our clothes off out in the woods in a sleeping bag, and I make him wait, or on Greg's porch where I let him move against me on the wicker couch. On the couch I make him keep on his underwear, and I make him wait. I know he's not going to keep waiting for too much longer, and even as we make out, I think about when I'll finally give in and let him have what he wants. But for right now, I make him wait.

I sit here listening to Greg going on and on about *fucking this* and *fucking that,* and I just sit here. I look out at the field and think about Ethan. Ethan never has to wait. Ethan never waits because nothing ever happens for Ethan. He doesn't do anything, and nothing ever changes. He'll just talk in his voices and watch TV and sleep in his white room forever until he dies. I get a feeling like ice poured into my stomach when I think about Ethan dying, which makes me think about the blue girl again as I'm watching Caroline bite her nails and Audrey look like she can't hold her head up, so I'm the one who finally says it.

O.K., I say. Let's go.

And then before I think about what I'm really saying, I tell Audrey we'll meet at her house and take her father's car, because her father's crazy and won't know, and it's too cold now to walk. Greg will drive, and we'll get into the car, all of us, and we'll go out to the lake and find her. I don't say it, but part of me thinks, *And then Greg will shut up about her once and for all.*

Because, really, I want to go, but more than that, I want Greg to stop talking about her.

Caroline says we shouldn't go, it's not right, we're going to get in a lot of trouble, which is what Caroline always says, and Greg says, *You and your fucking grades and your fucking tests,* and Caroline says, *At least I'm not failing fucking biology.* Caroline almost never curses, so we all laugh, even Audrey, whose mouth opens in a half-laugh, half-yawn. It makes me think of Ethan's mouth, how wide it is, how I can never make him close it all the way, how I wish he could be quiet, that he could just be. Greg looks over at me so quick I almost miss it. I can tell he's thinking about Ethan, too. Or at least I think he is. He has a certain look people seem to get when they think about Ethan. I know I shouldn't, but I get that look too, and I feel guilty about it. Maybe that's what makes me let Greg do whatever he wants.

I take out my mirror and put the lipstick on real slow, a big, deep circle. Greg is watching my mouth. It makes me want to laugh, the way he watches. I laugh a little too and get lipstick on my teeth and then wipe it away by curling my tongue. I laugh some more.

Greg says, *This is good. I can drive the fucking car. I'll drive it right out and find her.* He scrapes his sneakers on the cement. *The fucking lake. Now we're really going to fucking go.*

The others walk away when the bell rings. I try to count up all the fucks, but I lose count.

See you tonight, I say to Audrey, and she gives a little wave. We used to be so close, Audrey and me, passing notes to each other in class and laughing at all the same things. When we were little, we used to go to the lake with our mothers and pretend we were mermaids in the water, dragging ourselves along on our hands. Audrey never looks at me now. I talked to Greg about it, but he kept making those little sucking noises on my shoulder and said, *Audrey doesn't fucking look at anybody anymore. Audrey's a fucking freak.*

It made me a little mad when he said that, more than a little mad, and I thought about finding a way to get out there without him, out to the woods alone. Even though Mom is always driving off at night with her cakes and her friends, and even though my father hardly comes home, I am never alone. Maybe if I see the blue girl I'll be able to figure out how to really be alone.

At night, Greg comes for me and waits outside on the back lawn, out by the white fence that blocks out the trees. Everything on the lawn is framed in white. Even the flowers

Mom plants in the spring come up white. Sometimes when the sun hits, the trees look white, too. The fence keeps the trees out and Ethan in, so of course Ethan wants to run though the trees, run all the way out to the highway that leads to town. He wants to keep running until he makes it out to the lake, where he can scream and no one will hear him. I don't know if that's what Ethan really wants because there's no way to know, but this is what I think he wants, to run, to run and scream and have no one hear him. Because just like me, Ethan is never alone.

Caroline isn't with Greg when I open the sliding door and walk across the lawn. He brings his hands up to my face and kisses me with his slow tongue going around and around, and usually I kiss him back with my hands around his waist, but now I am too tired, tired of never being alone.

Where the fuck is Caroline? I ask, because it's what Greg would say.

He moves back and shoves his hands in his pockets. He laughs.

You shouldn't talk like that, he says, *you're too beautiful to talk like that.*

Now I'm the one who laughs.

Shut the fuck up, Greg, I say, because I want him to know how it feels to be on the other end of all those fucks. *Where's Caroline?*

I look up at my mom's window, at Ethan's window right next door, at the white moon in the sky, the white house, the white fence, all of it glowing. I pull my denim jacket around me and think, *This is the way I'll break out of all this white, by seeing the blue girl again, and up close,* but then I decide I'm not going. Not without Caroline, and definitely not without Audrey.

Greg says I should be cool, relax, that Caroline went to Audrey's, and we'll meet them there, and that he wanted some time alone with me, that he never gets any time alone with me, and he kisses me again, softer this time, until I give in to the complaining, give in to the kissing. When I'm done being kissed, I take his hand and lead him past the white gate, out to the road where we walk the white line holding hands. I look at the leaves and stuff my other hand in my pocket, and I think about how long the walk will take. Since we probably won't get to Audrey's until eight, I wonder if the blue girl will be asleep or if we'll have to wake her up, if she'll lie there waiting for me like she does when I see her in my mind, or if she'll come out to the road to find us, if she's been waiting for us all along.

By the time we get to Audrey's, my hands and face are colder than I remember them feeling in a long time. I have to make Greg stop pulling me over to the side of the road to touch me with his cold hands. I say, *Come on, already, you're the one who keeps saying you want to fucking see her,* and he says, *You shouldn't say fuck. I told you that you're too beautiful for that.*

Taking the car is easy. Audrey comes out with the keys and hands them to Greg without looking at him.

Are you sure your dad won't notice that his car is gone? I ask. And Audrey starts laughing hard, and says, *If only.* She points at the living room window. We can see right in. There's her father with the little ball in both hands, aiming it at the hoop. I tell Greg to open the car door because I don't want to see if he makes the shot or not.

The engine is quiet, and I tell Greg to drive slow, not to get crazy. Caroline reminds us that none of us has a license yet, that this is definitely against the law and that we could probably all get thrown out of school if we get pulled over. I don't even mind when he says, *Shut the fuck up, Caroline.*

We drive, all of us quiet, even Greg. At the spot in the woods where the road ends, Audrey says from the back seat, *Turn here.* It's the only thing anyone has said the whole way, and for a minute, while thinking about Ethan and his voices and the girl out there somewhere in the dark, I almost forget that Audrey is with us. I turn around to look at her, but Audrey doesn't look back at me. She looks really awake now, though, and she hasn't looked that way in a long, long time.

Greg turns down the road so hard the tires spin in the gravel, and I fall against the door. *Fucking road,* he says, and then squeezes my knee and mouths a *sorry.* It's so dark that even with the brights on we can't see anything, just trees and road and gravel. It's quiet in the car except for Greg muttering all of his *fucks* under his breath, and for a minute, I think I'm going to scream like Ethan. I'm just going to open my mouth as wide as it will go and scream for them to let me out when Audrey says, *Stop the car.*

Greg doesn't stop, so Audrey says it again, louder, then puts her hand on the back of his neck.

I said, stop the fucking car, she says.

Greg stops. The car shakes when he hits the brakes hard. *Take it easy, Audrey,* Greg says, and she tells him to stop telling her what to do.

You wanted to see her, right? she says. *Well, now you're going to.*

She opens the car door. The dome light goes on overhead. It's so dark even its faint light makes me squint. While I'm squinting, Audrey leans her head back into the car and looks right at me.

Stay here, she says. *Stay here until I tell you to come out.*

I nod at her. This time it's my turn to squeeze Greg's knee.

And turn off the lights, she says.

Caroline says to wait. *How is Audrey going to see in the dark? It's so dark out here,* she says, and she is breathing very hard when Audrey closes the door. She yells at Greg that he got us into this, that now something is going to happen to Audrey in the dark, and how are any of us going to be able to get her when we can't see her. Greg doesn't tell her to shut up again. He just shuts off the lights and that makes her quiet.

It's darker than I ever imagined it could be. I hold a hand up in front of my face, and it's true, I can't see it. I can't see Greg, who is moving his hand on my knee, squeezing, and then moving it up to my thigh. I try to follow Audrey, but she disappears in seconds. We are surrounded by trees, but it's too dark to see them.

For the longest time we sit. All we can hear is our own breath, mine and Greg's and Caroline's, all mixed so that I can't tell where my breath ends and Greg's starts.

Finally I can't take it. I can't stand all this breathing.

Where is she? I say. *Where is Audrey?*

I keep saying it, *Where's Audrey, where's Audrey?* and Greg tells me to calm down, but I'm beyond myself. It's like I've stepped out of my own skin and can see this girl sitting in a car with her friends, waiting to see this girl who may not even be there, who may not even be alive, and I look at the girl and want to tell her that it's time to stop all of this, all of it right now, this girl who may or may not be me. The girl in her white sweater and denim jacket is screaming, *Go get Audrey, we have to get Audrey right now,* this girl in the car who can't see anything, not even her hand in front of her face.

And then we hear something.

I don't wait. I open the car door and start running, the gravel flying up from my shoes, my mouth open and filling with hard, fast, burning breath. I can hear them behind me as they run, Caroline and Greg, but I won't stop now, can't stop, I just keep running in the thick dark with the gravel slipping and skidding under my shoes. Greg catches up and grabs my arm, and we keep running together until the gravel gives way to sand, and we're so close to the lake we almost run into it.

The girl is on her back. Audrey's hair is stuck to the sides of her head as she pulls the girl on her side and starts pounding her on the back. *Again, again, again,* is all I can think, flashing back to that day on the lake with our mothers, all three of them sitting there and not moving while Audrey did the work, and I move forward just a little like I'm really going to help her this time. But once again I just stand and watch as Audrey pounds. Water spits out from the girl's blue mouth. The air is full of coughing.

We stand looking down at her. It's hard to tell how blue she really is in all this darkness. Her eyes open, she looks up at us, and lifts her blue hand to her mouth to wipe away some of the water. Then she opens her mouth.

Fuck, Greg says, and backs away.

I keep looking at her, looking at the blue hand pointing to her open blue mouth and the small white teeth inside.

You saw her, Audrey says to Greg. *Now help me get her back to her house.*

Fuck that, Greg says. *No fucking way am I touching that,* and he starts moving back toward the car.

Caroline grabs his arm and says, *Where are you going, Greg? You can't leave us here,* and he says, *Fuck this, I'm getting back in the car.*

I think about what finally makes me move. Not the girl lying in front of us with her mouth open and staring. Not even Audrey, shivering in the cold. It's Ethan I think of, Ethan on the white tile with his mouth open, Ethan with his head pounding on the floor until it's bruised. What kind of a sister could I be to Ethan if I leave the blue girl all alone?

I try not to think of the weight of her on me as Audrey and I half-carry her back to the house. I try not to think about the darkness, or the way the girl's breath sounds up close, rattling, almost, and sharp. I try not to think about the house as we move closer to it, and I try not to think as I let Audrey go in by herself, and I stand outside in the gravel, trying not to wonder if she'll ever come out. I try not to think as we get back into the car. Caroline sits in the front with Greg, and I get in the back with Audrey and put my arm around her until she sinks against me. I try not to think about the wetness or the cold or the smell of the lake water in her hair. When Audrey gets out at her house, I stay in the backseat, alone, until Greg pulls me out.

Come on, we have to go now, her father will be looking for the car, he says. *Come on, I have to take you home.*

I let Greg help me out of the car. The shades are drawn, but still I can see her father's shadow. Part of me wants to watch while he plays his game, but I know I can't stay there in the driveway with Greg breathing all over me. I know I have to go home, and when I do, I will sit with my back against Ethan's door and listen to him talk to himself the way he does sometimes. *Ethan's O.K.,* he'll say, *Ethan's O.K. now.* Always the same, the way he says it. I think of the girl in the water and all that breathing and the sounds of the water spitting out of her mouth. I think about being home, sitting with my back against Ethan's door, whispering to Ethan four times, just the way he likes, that Ethan's right, that Ethan's O.K.

Irene

I WAS TRYING TO LISTEN TO THE TREES ON THE NIGHT they went to find her. It was all I could think to do. It's not that I didn't think of stopping them. It's not that I didn't know all along they would go. But the time for stopping them had passed. I realized that, sitting on the porch, hearing the garage door open and close, hearing their voices whisper.

I was sitting on the porch while Colin played his basketball game in the living room, after Buck had gone to bed in his sailboat pajamas, which have recently gotten short in the sleeves. I sat and tried to hear the operettas my mother talked about when I was a girl. My mother used to say that trees sang if you listened closely, so I would crane my neck toward the branches and dream of glissandos sung in voices that ached. When I told my mother I couldn't hear the trees, she said, *Keep trying, Irene, listen hard, listen deep,* but I thought the trees would never sing to me because their voices had been sucked away in a mass of pollen that made my sinuses ache. I could never be sure, but I always thought my mother left this world disappointed in me for missing out on those glorious voices. I keep sitting with the windows open listening for the trees' voices, but they don't speak to me.

But I did hear Audrey open and then quietly close her door. I didn't know she was awake, though I should have assumed it. Audrey, my Audrey, who never sleeps, my Audrey with circles under her eyes and that look of disdain.

The last time Magda, Libby, and I drove over to feed the girl, I tried to figure out what I had done to provoke Audrey's looks of disdain, but I had no answer. I knew only what I had not done. I took one of the moon pies in my hand and thought about how carefully I had baked the tops and the bottoms, and the careful spooning of the melted chocolate, the creamy richness of the filling, and I wondered if we will ever really be rid of the secrets.

I let my daughter save a dying girl, and I did nothing. That's one of my secrets, along with so many others. All secrets are terrible, I know that, and I know that no matter how many times I feed them to the blue girl, there is no relief.

I was sitting on the porch trying to hear the trees, but I was thinking of her, the girl in the bed, blue as a dream with her mouth full of wanting. I was trying to hear her breath echoing out from the lake when I heard the click of the car door closing, and I heard them drive off.

In the beginning we told each other the things we'd overheard, things our daughters whispered about a girl who lurked in their dreams. *Out by the lake,* they'd say. *She has no mother.* And then, *My God,* they'd say, *the girl is blue.*

We didn't believe them at first. We had sense enough then to turn our backs to the pieces of muffled conversation. We stopped short of reading their texts. *They're young, they're imaginative, they need something to believe,* we said to each other. In a town as dull as this one, it was what we needed. We could understand the boredom, the stifling we sensed in our girls, even at fifteen. We didn't want that for them, but what could we do? We had already long been broken.

I remember lying on the beach that afternoon, looking at Audrey while trying at the same time not to look because I knew if she caught me she'd turn away. I remember wondering if I had been that way with my own mother once, always distant, always trying to disappear, always dismissing her, she who had held me in her womb and squeezed me out. How ungrateful we all once were, we daughters who become mothers only to learn how it feels, the endless cycle of rejection. I remember thinking about my mother that day, wishing I could tell her how sorry I was.

For a moment, when I first saw the blue girl in the water, I actually thought she was my mother. For a moment I felt a choked sadness in my throat and wanted to call out to her, but then I looked at Audrey and knew that she had seen her, too.

There were no trees singing to us the first night that Magda, Libby, and I went to her. How tentative we were, slipping through the trees and out to the crook at the end of the road where the house sat, so alone, one bare window open. Magda and I held hands, and I remember thinking, *Try, Irene, try to hear the trees singing, try for your mother, you owe her that much.*

For a minute I thought I heard them, the trills of their voices, slow air blowing from rounded mouths, just the way trees ought to sound. I squeezed Magda's hand

and said, *I hear something,* and she said, *I do, too,* and then Libby knocked.

The old woman opened the door, peered at us, and shook her head, back and forth, back and forth, the way a child would, the way Buck does sometimes when he doesn't want to go to bed, when he sticks his fingers in his ears as if to tell me he will never hear me, that he has not only blocked out my voice with his fingers, but he has erased my voice forever.

Come at night, the old woman said. She hacked into a soiled handkerchief, her shoulders shaking as she coughed. *Only at night.*

She coughed again, a sputtering cough, and then looked directly at me. Her eyes were dark and heavy lidded. She hid her hands in her pockets.

Bring her something she can eat, the old woman said. *Something that you must give away.*

Magda rocked forward on her toes and said, *Like leftovers?* and the old woman laughed, her head thrown back as the coughing racked her shoulders and the back of her neck.

Something only she can have, she said, and then closed the door and disappeared into the house.

Libby stopped us at the edge of the road and said, *Let's bring her our secrets.*

We laughed, though it was not funny.

On the way home, I drove with the windows open and listened to the whistle of the trees. A whistle, not singing.

The only other thing I remember from that night is that I had a sudden and unmistakable craving for moon pies. I hadn't had that craving since I was pregnant, and just the thought of being pregnant—the way Audrey would turn inside me at night, the way Buck kicked so hard my bladder leaked—made me remember my poor mother, and that I will never be the kind of woman who can hear the singing of the trees.

I go inside. Colin is sitting with the Nerf ball in his hand, tired from the end of his game. He doesn't ask what I am doing up or why I've been sitting out in the cold air. He never asks where I've gone when Magda and Libby and I go to the girl's house. He never asks about the smell of chocolate and vanilla. He never asks why the dishes remain in the sink after midnight, or why I slip onto the sofa bed out on the porch and lie alone under woolen blankets, smoking cigarettes ten years after quitting. But I imagine him asking, in the quiet way he had in the early years of our marriage, and I imagine turning to him and saying, *I need to feel it, Colin, I need the smoke to fill me. The air is not enough.*

I think about what it was like in July, how Colin sat for three weeks in front of the television in a crash position, arms locked over the top of his head, his body curling into itself the way school children are taught to shield themselves if a bomb were ever to fall. For three weeks he would not leave the television unguarded, until I called the ambulance, and they took him away, and the doctors threw him into a haze of medication and half-dreams of men who feel things too deeply, only to end up not feeling at all.

Now he plays his private games in the living room with a Nerf ball and a hoop screwed over the door. He shoots, misses, shoots again. Sometimes he catches me watching him from the doorway and turns his back to me, sitting in a chair and moving his hand up and down with the ball, pretending to dribble, and then hoisting the ball over the couch, sending it sailing above the pictures of our children on the end tables, and scoring.

I used to think, when he first came home and the sun was still hot, about walking across the living room to him, taking his hand, and walking together out the back door all the way to the edge of the lawn where the lake shimmers in the distance at night. I used to imagine sitting on the lawn with ice clinking in our glasses of Scotch and soda, and then, slowly and methodically, without hurt or recriminations, retracing our steps into the past to find out how we got here. I'd tell him about that day in the lake, about the light on the water, about the blue girl almost drowning, about all the blueness I've felt since that day. I'd tell him that the blue girl is really here, and so are we.

As I stand in the doorway and watch him there with the Nerf ball, I know that it's not how we got here that matters. It's that we are here, now.

Colin, I say, *how was your game?*

Of course Colin doesn't answer. Colin never answers.

I think of telling him they took his car, the car he no longer drives. But I don't. I think of driving out to find them. But I don't. I go to the kitchen and start separating egg whites, mixing in sugar and butter and cream and vanilla. I look out the window at the street lights and think of how I have become the kind of woman who does nothing, how I have become the kind of woman who bakes strange little pies, who knows her daughter has gone out into the woods but has done nothing to stop her.

The moon pies were finished by the time Audrey came home. Colin had started a new game. When Buck coughed several times, I stood in the doorway of his room for a while, looking down at him in his sailboat pajamas.

Audrey? he said, but when he saw me standing there watching him, he says, *Oh, I thought you were Audrey,* and went back to sleep, turning his back to me.

When I heard the car, I turned off the kitchen lights and stood by the window. After I'd spooned the melted chocolate over the pies, I'd opened the window to release the smell, and for a while I just stood there with my arms folded against the chill of the night air, trying to hear the singing.

My mother would not have understood. I could feel her disappointment leaking over me in a thick film, even over my hands, sticky from the filling and chocolate.

I let Audrey slip into the house and head to the bathroom, while I stood in the dark listening to the sound of her washing, the sound of her opening and closing her bedroom door, and the sound of her small television warming up. For a long time I waited, and then I tapped on the door.

I said her name, low. She opened her eyes and stared.

I'm up, she said. *I'm always up.*

She rolled away from me. I saw her clothes, balled and wet on the floor, but I said nothing. What was there that could be said?

The next morning, I make a sandwich for Buck to take school while he and Audrey whisper in the dining room.

Audrey will not bring lunch anymore, and I've given up trying to feed her.

Hurry up, I hear Audrey say, *before Mom comes.*

I see Buck balancing a bag of sugar on the top of his head and moving from side to side, back and forth, side, back, side again. Here is my eight-year-old son holding his arms out in front of him as if holding the body of a woman.

Doing the waltz, again? Audrey asks.

Buck smiles. *You'll make me lose count,* he says, as he dances around the room.

I turn back to the kitchen, wrap his sandwich in cellophane, and stuff it into a paper bag. *Time to go,* I call.

Bucks straps himself into the backseat, and Audrey sits beside me in front. Her eyes are heavy lidded, the sockets deep and lined as if she's been bruised. I don't ask why the undersides of her eyes look so blue. I know where she's been.

Didn't you sleep well? I ask.

She keeps her face averted. Buck kicks the back of my seat.

I didn't sleep, she says.

We stop at the traffic light in front of the grammar school. Boys with heavy backpacks rush across the street as the crossing guard holds up her white-gloved hand.

She smiles at me and waves as we pull forward into the school driveway.

I'll see you at three o'clock, I say to Buck, already halfway out the door. I roll down the window when I see the paper bag on the front seat.

Buck! I call. *Buck!* and as I call his name I feel a knot in my throat, a tightness so deep I think I might lose my breath. He looks so small against the brick building and the open sky above it. I want to ask for a kiss, I want to pull him back into the car and drive away with him, but I don't. I dangle the bag and say, *Don't forget your lunch, honey,* and he says, *Thanks, Mom,* in a voice so sweet my ribs ache.

He holds his sandwich bag on top of his head and twirls around. Audrey laughs.

I say nothing. I let them have their secret. Now, I think, we all have them.

We drive past the road to the woods where the blue girl lives. Audrey doesn't look at me, not once, though I watch her as we wind our way through town, past the lake, past the place where the girl drowned. The only thing she ever told me, the one thing she allowed herself to say that night when it was all over, when we were home again, when we sat together on the sofa drinking tea, was that her lips had been warm.

Who would ever think, she'd said, *that lips like that could ever feel warm?*

I think of the feeling of the girl's lips when she licked the filling out of my hand. The lips were so warm.

Audrey, my beautiful Audrey, who is getting so thin, who saved a girl from drowning when everyone was too frightened to move. Audrey, who saved the girl who eats secrets too terrible to share. Audrey, who gave the girl her own breath as if it was a blessing.

Everyone asks her, Magda tells me. *Everyone wants to know. So many questions, but she won't tell.*

Are you making your moon pies again? she asks.

The question startles me. I adjust the rearview mirror and press my lips together to blot my lipstick.

For the bake sale, I lie, *to help raise money for scholarships so those summer kids don't end up running our town.*

In all the years I have lived in this sorry town, I can't remember a single a bake sale, not one. We've certainly never set up tables at the lake to sell to the summer people, who flee as soon as the days grow shorter and who leave us with our husbands, who no longer look at us in our bathing suits in the summer or pour us cocktails in the early autumn evenings.

I wish she'd allow me the tiniest of lies. I wish she would not try to know my secrets. But Audrey is wise. Wise enough to jump into the water and pump water out of a blue girl's lungs. Wise enough to smile at her father and his basketball games and pick up his Nerf ball if he misses. Wise enough to hold her brother when he can't get to sleep and I am too distracted to help. Wise enough to take her father's car and go to the blue girl without me.

O.K., Mom, she says. *For the bake sale. O.K.*

She opens the door and slides one leg out, letting the toe of her shoe touch the ground. She swings her foot back and forth against the pavement, making a soft scraping sound that makes me think of my mother and her hope that I would hear the singing trees. The branch of a tree casts a shadow over us. I hear my mother urging me to listen, but it's as if my ears have been stopped up. Audrey's eyes shine as she looks past me, past the parking lot and the school and all of the things that make up this town.

She could do it again, you know, she says without looking at me. *I think she wants to do it again.*

I want to lay my hands on hers and squeeze them, squeeze the fingers that are ringed with my mother's freckles. I want to close the doors and hold her hands and lift them against my heart so she can feel it beating. I want to tell her that I know where she's been and that I have been there too. I want to tell her about the nights I've gone out to the lake with Magda and Libby, about the girl's lips warmer than I'd ever have imagined, about the smell of the sweet pies and the way we've fed her. I want to squeeze her hands and lead us into a song for my mother, a song we'll sing with the windows closed, a song we'll sing past the lake, down the long road and away from this town.

Audrey gets out of the car. Before she turns away, she looks back at me with her eyes red and swollen, the irises clouded by lack of sleep. I open my mouth to sing out her name as I watch her move away, but as I do, I feel my throat turn thick with a sadness that will not allow me to speak. I sit in the driver's seat and watch her walking farther and farther away from me, until the doors of the school open and close, and she has gone inside, in her world free of all this blueness.

Audrey

MY MOTHER KNOWS.

I can see it just by looking at her, the way she stares at me, the way she came in my room last night and stood there like I didn't know what she wanted. When she says good-bye to me in the car, I think of just saying it to her. I think of telling her that we "borrowed" Dad's car and that I found her, face down in the lake, just like I knew I would. I think of telling her that I jumped in and put my mouth right over hers and breathed into her. Again.

Again and again and again.

Just like the nights of not sleeping, of lying there and thinking I can't take it another second, that I'm going to jump out of bed and run all the way out to the road and into the woods where no one can find me, not even her.

Her. Her. Her.

She's all I think about. If I ask myself why should I get in the car and go to her again, when I know what I'll do once I get there, I don't have an answer. Except that there's been something connecting us since that day, since I breathed into her mouth and she breathed back into mine. And that's all I can say about it.

The only thing that keeps me from screaming is Buck. I would never want to scare Buck, Buck with his crazy dreams and the bag of sugar on his head. He's too little for dreams like those. He's too little to have a sister who would wake him up with her screaming if she didn't deliberately keep herself from going crazy. He's too little to have a mother making moon pies and pretending she's not going out to a lake to feed a girl who's blue. And he's too little for a father who does nothing but play basketball by himself with a Nerf ball and a little hoop.

The night we went out to the lake, Buck came into my room and stood by my bed.

Audrey, he said, *Audrey, are you up?*

I just looked at him and said, *Don't you know by now I'm always up?*

He gave me a sad look, sadder, even, than his too-tight pajamas with the sailboats on them. I felt my throat go tight when he looked at me that way.

Next time, he said, *next time, promise you'll take me with you.*

With me where? I said, and then, *Buck, don't get any ideas about where I've been.*

I pulled myself up and leaned on my elbows.

There won't be any next time, I said. *You have to go back to bed.*

He nodded and opened the door. Through the opening I could see the Nerf ball whizzing by, our father bending down to pick up the ball after he missed.

Take me next time, he said, and then closed the door before I had a chance to answer him.

I am so tired. The tiredness makes my arms and hands itch. It makes my stomach squeeze. Every minute of every day I am one giant blur of tired.

But when I found her and breathed into her last night, for the first time since that day at the lake, I didn't feel tired. I felt huge again. Enormous. Like she had blown something into me that made me expand. Even my jeans felt tight.

The whole way home, while Rebecca was rubbing my wet back, I wanted to tell her about the feeling, the way I would have when we were younger, before she started messing around with Greg, before she got almost too pretty to talk to. I wanted to tell her that I opened my mouth and breathed something in, something huge and whole and mine.

If I could, I would share it, but somehow, whatever this is, this huge thing inside me that I carry around, this thing that makes me dream even when I can't sleep, it seems to be mine alone. Sometimes at night when the television's on, I think of sharing the feeling with Buck, of putting my mouth on his and breathing into him while he's asleep, but the thought is so disgusting that I lie awake all night in a sweat. Sometimes I think of trying to give whatever it is to my father, because if anyone needs to wake up, it's him. Sometimes I think of giving it to Ethan, but then, what would he do with it? Probably the only peace you get inside a head like Ethan's, a head full of weird voices and cartoons, is during sleep.

Every time I've seen her, she's been awake. Her eyes are always open. Even when I found her facedown in the water, just the way I did in the half-dream I've had too many nights to count, her eyes were open. *Fixed is actually the right word,* I think. When I turned her over and pushed the air out of my lungs and breathed into her mouth, she smiled like she'd been expecting me all along.

It's not that I minded being awake, not at first. After I pulled her out of the lake in front of my mother and her friends, the days were long, and there seemed to be so much to do. I'd sit in the living room after Buck and my mother went to bed, and I'd watch my father play basketball by himself in the living room. He seemed to like it when I watched, the way I'd watched the TV set with him when he thought it was going to blow up. For those first three weeks we just sat together, me and my father, me on the couch with my feet up and under a blanket, even though it was still so hot out, and my father on the floor in front of the TV with his hands over his head.

It's all right, Dad, I said to him one night when he kept getting up and pacing around the room and then crouching down again. *Nothing's going to happen.*

He said, *Yes, something will happen, Audrey,* and he sat back down on the floor and rocked.

That was the last time he really looked at me, the night before Mom made the call, before they took him away.

The next day Buck and I stood at the window and watched him go. One of the men in the ambulance put his hand on my father's shoulder. He went with his head down, kicking at the gravel in the driveway like a little kid. Buck asked where Dad was going, and I said, *Someplace good, someplace safe. A place where he won't have to worry so much.* My mother got in the ambulance with him but didn't cry. None of us cried, though I think we should have.

Buck said, after he was gone, *Does this mean we can watch TV again?* and I said yes, and then he asked if this meant that things would go back to the way they were, when Dad was O.K., and I said they would, but I knew it wouldn't be O.K. again, even then, even before that first time I saved her life, even before I lay here night after night, unable to sleep.

Last night I hid my balled-up wet clothes in the back of my closet after my mother peeked in, then turned around and left, closing the door behind her. I knew she wouldn't look. I knew she wouldn't ask about the wet clothes or why I was shivering or why I took so many towels from the linen closet. She knew we took the car, but she wouldn't ask who drove or where we went. As I put on my nightgown, I started thinking we should be a lot more careful, that letting Greg drive was a bad idea, that maybe Caroline was right and we should just stay away and let our mothers do whatever they were going to do. But we can't stay away. Greg is definitely going to go again. I can feel it in every fuck he says, every *fucking blue girl* this and *fucking blue girl* that. *What did she ever do to you?* I'd asked in the car on the way out to the lake, and he'd said, *Why the fuck do you care so much about a fucking blue girl anyway?*

After I'd saved her, again, Greg didn't say a word. When he parked Dad's car in the driveway and turned out the lights, I asked, *Why do* you *care about her so much, Greg?*

Yeah, just shut the fuck up now, Greg, Rebecca said as she opened the door, and then everyone went quiet. I got out of the car and walked away with Dad's keys in my hands and the blue girl's breath inside me.

When I know my mom has gone out to the porch to smoke her cigarettes, I sit down on the living room rug to watch my father play. He looks very tired but doesn't stop playing. I think maybe that if I can watch him long enough, my father catching and throwing and catching, maybe I'll be able to doze off for at least a little while. The longer I watch him, though, the less tired I become. My throat feels sore from helping her breathe, my chest going up and down, up and down. I keep seeing her face in the back of my eyelids every time I close them.

He stops dribbling for a minute and stares at the hoop.

Are you winning, Dad? I ask him.

He seems surprised to hear me talk to him, as if my voice itself is a surprise. We look at each other, me and my father, as if we've never seen each other before. I wonder how I look to him now, now that I don't sleep, with her blueness inside me.

He doesn't answer. I lie on the rug all night watching him not winning.

Magda

LIKE I TOLD IRENE, WE SHOULD HAVE KNOWN. THESE kids with their ideas. It was only a matter of time before they went looking for her. *It's not like the moon pies don't leave a smell,* I said when Irene called me after finding Audrey's wet clothes. *It's not like we've been so good about hiding it. We make pies and go out in the night. They were bound to figure us out. Look at my boy, Greg,* I said, *always watching me stir the chocolate. You can't hide much from kids, Irene.* I wanted to add that everyone knows that her husband is not right in the head and that she should stop being ashamed. Caroline has told me about the strange games he plays with a basketball, and that he thinks the TV will blow up one day and kill them all.

Look at Ethan, I said, and that is enough. Any time we feel our problems clogging our heads like water in the ears, that's all we have to say.

Look at Ethan.

Before the girl came, we all looked at Ethan. We pitied. We wrapped our arms around Libby's shoulders when she talked about the school filled with kids who wear helmets, kids who can't go to the bathroom on their own. We saw the small yellow bus. We saw him getting bigger and still talking in that voice of his. We knew.

It's not that we'd forgotten Ethan once the girl came, but our pity has changed. Shifted. Now, we don't look at him so much. Me, I've always been a little bit afraid of him, which is something, as a mother, I hate to admit, but now that the blue girl has come, now, after all the feedings, we haven't been thinking as much about Ethan with his strange voice and flat ears. Libby doesn't say as much, but I suspect she feels more at ease now, too, without all of us looking all the time at her son.

Which of course, Mama would say, *must be a feeling so terrible. You should feel more, Magdalena,* she'd say. *You are not feeling as much for others as you did when you were a girl. Feeling is something you should do.*

After I hung up with Irene, I started on the pies. It wasn't really a decision or a plan—I just started taking out the cookie sheet and the mixing bowl, the marshmallow cream and the chocolate, without even thinking. *I feel things, Mama,* I wanted to say. I feel the need to feed her, deep in my middle, and I hear Mama's laughter in my head.

You who always hated cooking, she'd say. *Now look at you in a sea of mixing bowls.*

They come home while I start to make the pies, and I'm filling the kitchen with my smells, as if Mama and I are alone in the kitchen, melting the chocolate for the cookie tops and bottoms, though Mama would never have eaten moon pies. *Too sweet,* she'd have said, *and the filling sticks in the gut.*

Caroline comes in first, always, and flops herself down at the table. I notice she's late today, but I don't let on. There are still things I keep to myself. All mothers do.

Caroline begins to talk as I put the cookies for the tops and the bottoms of the moon pies in the oven. *The things that house the secrets,* I think. She is a talker, my girl, always full of words. I imagine her head like the ticker on the news shows with a stream of neon words running across, never stopping, eventually repeating. She was young when she started talking, fourteen months, and she has not stopped since. When she was little, I sometimes used to pray she'd stop talking so much, always jabbering, always *Mama this* and *Mama that.* My own Mama warned me how I would come to miss the sound of my own name, my name disappearing into a sea of *Mamas.* How right she was.

I love Audrey, Caroline says, picking at a page in one of the many books she is always carrying, *but Audrey's family is kind of strange.*

Right away she starts on about Audrey, and I think, *She will tell, she will have to tell. How I love this girl for being the kind who tells.*

I open a carton of eggs and say, *Live long enough, my girl, and you'll find out how strange everyone is. All of us.*

Greg appears in the kitchen. It's as if one day the stomping ended and this is what the boy does now. He appears. He startles me, but I don't show it as I set the chocolate squares in the pot and start melting them.

He must have overheard our conversation because he picks up where we left off. *Audrey's the fucking strangest of all,* he says. *Audrey's seriously fucking strange.*

And I say, *You, boy, have nothing to say about weirdness in this house. You stole a fucking car.*

He says, *How the fuck do you know that?*

I watch the chocolate start to bubble and stir it while they watch me.

I told you before, I say, *I have my ways.*

Then I tell him to get out of my kitchen before I ground him for the rest of his life, this boy who steals cars and messes around with Rebecca in the woods behind the house and out on the back porch. I think about all those nights standing out in the lake when I was their age, David and I with our hands and mouths all over each other and that is why I stayed in this town, because of that lake and those hands. It all started there, and I don't want either one of them to end up like that. Caught. Caught in a lake or in the woods or in a car stolen from a man who cannot drive because he fears his own television.

Plus the boy, this boy of mine, is failing biology, which is the one thing I wish he understood right now.

Caroline sits at the table and opens her notebook as I lower the flame on the stove and crack egg whites into a bowl and pour in the vanilla and sugar and set to mixing. Her hair has gotten longer all of a sudden. I didn't see it happen, even though I've been watching. She looks softer, my girl. It's clear I need to pay more attention. I wish she would smile more, show off those beautiful teeth. If Mama were here, she would get Caroline to smile. But I don't have a way with a joke the way Mama did, and Caroline's teeth are the last thing I should be thinking about when those kids are out there stealing cars. Libby, she has to worry about teeth, with Ethan and his biting, but I have a boy who has hands that move, hands that can do things, hands that are a cause for worrying.

Right now I want no worries. I want to assemble the moon pies.

As if reading my mind, Caroline closes her notebook and says, *I'm worried about Audrey.*

Well, I say, putting down the mixer, *Audrey is someone to worry about.*

I check on the tops and the bottoms of the moon pies and wait for Caroline to talk. If there's one thing I learned from Mama, it's to act distracted. The trick is to not actually be distracted, and this is where I make my mistake. But still I try. I keep on with the mixing and the stirring and the spooning, and then I think about her, out there in the house, waiting. I can feel the rumble of her breath, her mouth always open.

And then Caroline is talking again. Whispering.

What? I ask, looking up from the bowl.

I said we went out there, she says.

Her hair falls in front of her face. I try to think what Mama would do at a time like this. *Be soft,* she would say, *you with the hard edge, why so hard all the time? This girl is one who needs softness.*

Mama would be right. *Not so brittle,* she would say. *A time and a place there is for everyone to be brittle, not now. Now is a time for soft.*

I walk over to the kitchen table where Caroline is sitting with her head down, hair falling forward. I wish I had one of the butterfly clasps she wore for weeks, even though she looks so much better without them. Softer.

I think of Mama and place one hand under her chin to lift it toward me, then smooth the hair back with the palm of my hand. *See, Mama, not so bad,* I think, as I hold the hair back with my fingers.

So you saw her, I say to Caroline. *So tell me.*

And she does. She tells me about the car and Greg with Rebecca in front, about the dark trees and about the road, the road I know so well, the one leading up to the house. She tells me about the gravel spraying up under the car and the way the trees seemed to come down around them. *Like they were going to envelop us,* she says—her word, *envelop,* my girl with the ever-expanding list of words that will one day get her out of this town. She tells me about the sound of the water and Audrey running in the dark, about the girl in the water, face down, Audrey pounding again on her back. She tells me that Rebecca was the one to help Audrey to the door of the house with the girl's arm around her, how Audrey shivered the whole way home and said nothing, just like her father.

I take my time when she is done.

So you saw her for yourself, I say.

I take a breath and smell the cookies cooling in the air. David will be home soon, asking about dinner, what I am doing with these cakes, as he calls them. I just need to be fast enough, fast enough with the plates and the dinner on the table, and then later in bed, with the television still on, I will be fast with my hands on him, always moving, moving so fast he hardly knows where I've been or whether I'm there or gone.

The trick, I once told Irene and Libby in a moment of embarrassment, *is to move so much he hardly knows when you're gone. To know how to keep him breathless.*

When Irene looked away and Libby said she'd settle for just knowing her husband was still breathing, I knew I had said the wrong thing. But who else is there to talk to?

Her. There is the girl.

I need to finish up with Caroline before Greg comes back in and David pulls into the driveway and it starts, the stuff of families. I pour the chocolate onto the cookies and hope they will cool in time.

But you saw her already that day at the lake, I tell her, hurrying now. *You saw her that day with Audrey. Just because we don't say it doesn't mean it didn't happen.*

I touch her hand then. *You see, Mama?* I think. *I can still be soft.*

Her lips part then, showing just the thinnest line of those beautiful teeth, and her chin moves up and down, fast. It takes me a minute to realize she is trying not to cry.

It's not that I didn't believe, she says. *It's just that everyone is talking. Especially Greg.* She stops and sniffles. *He just kept saying he was going out there to get her. But it was Rebecca who said we should do it, like she didn't believe, and then I thought maybe I didn't, either. Maybe it never happened, that day. So I went,* she says.

And what did you see? I ask.

She looks straight at me then. I reach up to wipe her tears with my fingers, rubbing them together in circles. I don't want to get up, but I must have forgotten to rinse the pot because what's left of the chocolate is starting to burn.

I didn't, she says. *All I saw was Audrey. It was so dark that all I saw was Audrey running past. I didn't see her at all.*

The chocolate has singed the bottom of the pot, part of a set of cookware that's almost twenty years old, a gift from my parents when we got married. *For you to cook for that lanky boy,* Mama said, as if that was all I would ever do, all he would ever be. What strange dreams Mama had for me.

I pull Caroline by the hand and bring her over to the stove with me, holding her right hand down on the counter with one of mine, while I spoon what is not burned of the chocolate onto the last of the cookies that make up the tops and bottoms of the moon pies. She tries to pull away from me, but I hold her hand there against the counter, hard enough for her not to walk away, not even with the stink of burnt chocolate in the air. We stand there looking down at the burn marks on the pot, me and this girl child I call my own, this girl of mine with a head filled with words and too much softness, looking at the thick black ring on the old pot.

You didn't see her? I say.

I am whispering now. Mama would not believe how soft I've become.

Not really, I told you, it was too dark, she says.

Now she is pulling her hand away. I let it go.

Good, I say. *It's not somewhere you should go, out there. You or Audrey, either. Don't listen to Greg. He has ideas.*

The telephone rings and rings. I hear the sound of my own voice on the answering machine, and then a click. I know it is Irene.

Audrey was the one who saved her, Mama, she says. *I didn't do anything. I swear. It was Audrey.*

I realize I'm still holding the burnt pot in my hand. *I should throw it out,* I think, *buy new, or maybe*—and this is the first time I've thought this—*stop making the pies. Stop the feeding.* But the girl would starve, and the girl has done nothing except to be herself, blue as she is. It is we who have failed, we who have had to turn to the baking of these little pies. Then there is poor Audrey, always saving the girl, Audrey who cannot sleep.

Listen to me this one time, I say. *Just this one time. If you never listen to me again about anything,* I say, my hand shaking around the handle of the pot, *then fine, but this one time, you need to listen.*

I always listen, she says, and I can see by the line in her lips and the movement in her chin that the tears may come again.

Don't go out there again, I say.

O.K., she says. She's stopped herself from crying. O.K.

Promise, I say.

She promises. She is a good girl. I hug her, and in the hugging I forget I still have the pot in my hands. As my one arm comes around I think that Mama is right, that I've lost my softness, the softness that all mothers should have, the kind I used to have, too, and that Mama was not one to hug, and neither am I. We have that in common.

The top of the pot lands on the floor, the burnt chocolate spattering in thick blobs of dark brown.

What the fuck was that? Greg yells from the other room.

He appears then in that new way of his, his big feet and freckled arms hanging down in my line of vision as I take up the pot and bring it over to the sink, running water.

Ma, he says, coming to hover as I scour the burnt section of the double boiler with a Brillo pad. *What the fuck is that smell?*

I put down the pot in the sink and fill it with water that would scald my hands if I touched it. I think of the two of them when they were small, how I always kept them far from the stove, saying, *Hot, hot,* in that voice we mothers all learn to use. I've always warned them not to touch the things in my kitchen, the things that are too hot. Now everything feels that way, heated up. Scalding.

Before he can step away from me, because I am too fast for him—this boy has taught me to be fast, faster than he is—I wrap my hand around the back of his neck and lean into his ear.

I want to tell him I know what he's doing, that I know they sneak out to the porch at night, that I've seen the looks and the hands that are no longer in pockets fumbling around because there is someone else to touch now, that I was young once, too, and filled with heat, with yearning, with hunger.

But there is no time to say any of this, thinking about the hunger, because I can feel it inside myself now, pulling me out of the kitchen, out to the woods and to the girl, as if she alone is calling me.

Look at this fucking pot, I say, which makes the boy laugh.

Jesus, Ma, he says, *what the fuck did you do to it?*

I laugh, too, for a minute, and so does Caroline, the three of us laughing in the kitchen while my moon pies are setting on the cooling rack and Irene and Libby are soon to be out at the woods waiting for me.

It's my pot, boy, I say, *and what I do with it is none of your fucking concern.*

Neither of them says anything. Greg, the boy who held me here all those years ago, the boy with the freckled arms who has become lanky like his father, with hands always moving, has nothing to say. Even Caroline has no words. Her mouth is open.

The two of them stand there watching me as I race around the room, putting away the mixer, cleaning the measuring spoons and the bowl, grinding the eggshells in the garbage disposal. Then I stand there and assemble the moon pies, one after the other, pressing them gently with my hands, careful not to let the filling squeeze from the sides and break them apart.

Caroline

I *PROMISED*. THAT'S THE FIRST THING I THINK WHEN I get upstairs and on the computer. Mama asked me to promise, and I did. But I don't know if it's a promise I can keep.

Mama did not swear she would stop going. Why should I promise if she won't? Why should Mama be the only one to see her?

I start clicking. I move the mouse and click and breathe, in and out, in and out, trying to feel if there's a wheeze in my chest, too, if there's a pulmonary obstruction, because I suddenly feel like coughing for a long time until I can't cough anymore, until there's no air left inside me.

Until I turn blue. Like her. Because who's to say, really, that I couldn't? Maybe there was a time when she wasn't blue. Maybe she was once like us, like me, just a girl with too many thoughts and too many words who one day coughed and coughed and coughed herself blue.

It could happen, I think, as I click and cough, cough and click. It could happen to me. It could happen to any of us. Except Audrey. Audrey, I think, is now above becoming blue. Impervious to it. Audrey has had her mouth on the girl's mouth twice now. Twice she's saved her, and you'd think, you'd really think that kind of contact would turn anyone blue, if anything could. But not Audrey. There is something different about Audrey since the girl came and Audrey started saving her. Maybe I have it wrong altogether. Maybe Audrey's the one most likely to turn blue.

I click. I click and click and click.

`See bluish coloration`

`Rapid onset of wheezing`

`Pulmonary obstruction`

`Chronic coughing`

I click and think, click and cough, click and think and cough some more. There has to be a better word for blue skin. There just has to. But how to describe her? I close my eyes and try to see the flash of her moving past the car and into the lake, but I didn't get a good look. After all that, after Greg kept on with all the fucks and even Rebecca told him to stop, all I remember is the splash.

Inky, I think. I type it in and hold my breath.

`Inky skin`

It comes back:

`No results for inky skin. Consider narrowing your search.`

I type in new searches and click and click and click on them, each one, until the lists gets longer and longer.

Then I try:

`Signs of death`

I cough some more. Then I try:

`Signs of impending death`

It's a word I like. *Impending.* That's how everything feels now, like the whole world is impending.

`There are two phases of death: the pre-active and the active phase. In the pre-active phase, the patient may appear confused or detached. Conversation may become impossible. Patient may begin to refuse visitors, even loved ones, during this phase, and may also refuse food and drink.`

But she still eats moon pies. This I know.

I click on `active phase.`

`When a patient moves into the active phase of dying, the skin of the extremities or torso area often turns bluish (see` *`mottled skin`*`). The nail beds may also appear blue, as will the lips and area surrounding the mouth. Oxygen pools to the major organs` (heart, lungs, liver) and may cause the skin to appear blue or even purple.

The smell of the burnt chocolate keeps coming from downstairs as I sit at the screen and read it over and over. I wish I could have seen her up close, the way Audrey has, but it was so dark that night in the woods with the headlights off and the lake all around us, everything black, not blue. I try to picture what she looked like when she came out of the water, but all I saw was Audrey with her arm around the girl, Audrey's hair wet and stuck to her face. It was so dark in the car, so dark I could hardly breathe, so dark my throat felt thick the way it does when I'm nervous, when Mama goes out to the girl, or when Greg and Rebecca are out on the porch making sounds they think no one can hear. It makes my throat tight just looking at the word—`dying`—and I click away from the site and shut the computer down. I lie on my bed and try to calm it all down: my breathing, the need to cough, knowing someone in my own town is blue and may be dying, and knowing that Mama has joined up with the mothers of my best friends, and they're all making moon pies to keep the girl from dying.

Is that what Mama is doing? I wonder. Is that why she makes the pies? Is she trying to keep her alive? Or it is something else?

I promised I wouldn't go. I did promise.

I wonder how it feels to die. To be dying. To be dying and not even have anyone know you're dying.

At least I don't worry as much about my brain anymore. Now it's respiration, rates of breath, the oxygen level in my blood. Now I hardly think of my convolutions or synaptic firings or which parts of my brain control the involuntary response, because now I see that it's all so involuntary. Now I know I can't hold my breath long enough to die.

I think about Mr. Davis's lecture on complex thought and cognitive skills, the impairments that are a result of oxygen deprivation or the failure of chromosomes to meet. Maybe the blue girl has something chromosomal, like Ethan. Maybe I'm thinking about it all wrong. How can I know if I'm right if I haven't really seen her?

I should tell someone, I think, as I get up from my bed. *I should tell someone that we could all be wrong, all of us, our mothers and their secret visits, and even Audrey, who dives into the water.*

But who?

At dinner I eat only salad, even though Mama has made lamb chops and scalloped potatoes, green beans sautéed with almonds, and artichoke hearts dipped in olive oil. The kitchen is filled with her cooking, which I know is a sign of Mama's nervousness because this is the kind of meal she makes when she goes off with her friends and the moon pies.

I am not fooled. I chew the tri-color salad slowly. I swish the tomato seeds around my teeth, then the cucumbers crunch into nothing but water, and for a minute I hope I don't suffer from diverticulitis with all these seeds. My grandmother had it, the one from Russia. After meals she'd lie on the couch and say, *Oh, sweet girl with the beautiful teeth, in Russia we didn't have so many seeds to stick in the gut. Bring me a piece of bread.* She'd lie on the couch and chew the bread I brought. Crumbs would fall from her mouth. *This bread is so good I could die for it. People die for less, you know, much less.*

I'd nod and she'd chew some more.

For bread I would die, she'd say, *but not for seeds. Why in America are there so many seeds?*

I reach for a piece of bread and eat it without butter, letting my mouth go dry as I think of my grandmother with the seeds lining the pockets in her intestines.

My father eats and eats. Each jab of his fork brings a smile to his face, he and Greg always laughing, laughing at the food, even as Greg says, *Ma, this is a fucking feast,* and my father loses some of the scalloped potatoes as they spray out of his mouth and he says, *Watch it with all the fucks, boy, your mother doesn't like it,* and Mama says from her place at the sink, where she scrubs that pot with the burnt chocolate, *You've got that fucking right.* Then they all laugh. All except me.

After dinner Mama is still scrubbing her pot at the sink. I go over to help her.

Mama, I say, *maybe you should give up on that pot.*

She smiles and drops the Brillo pad in the sink.

Caroline, my girl, there are things you can't understand. This was a gift from my mother. How can I just throw it away? You can't throw away things given to you from the dead. They're all you have left.

I know there's something more about that pot, because Mama is not really so sentimental. She misses my grandmother, I know that, but if my grandmother were here and she saw that blackened pot, she'd tell my mother to stop holding on. Mama's proud of me, I know that too, but once, when I couldn't remember what grade I'd gotten on a paper and started crying because I couldn't find it, she had to admit she'd thrown the paper away. Not just that one, but all of them.

I throw them out, she told me, *so that boy, that brother of yours, doesn't cheat,* she said.

But I knew better.

And that's how I feel as I decide to break the promise while standing in the kitchen with the scalloped potatoes and the burnt pot, with my father and Greg watching television in the next room, with my mother scrubbing and scrubbing and waiting to be alone. I feel that I know better.

While she's still scrubbing, I feel this hunger deep inside, and it's not because I only ate the salad and need to diet because my waist is getting so *thick*—as Mama says—or because I'm afraid to die right there in the kitchen—who's to say I won't?—but because I want something. I want something I cannot name, something that will pull me out of the books and words and my own head, something that will take me out to where they've been.

To her.

I wait and wait until Mama stops scrubbing and has to go into the living room because my father is calling. I hear them talking about Greg and Rebecca, Mama asking my father if he knows what's going on, and my father saying, *They're just kids, like we were once.* Mama says, *Don't you remember what happened to us? Do you want him to be trapped?* My father tells her that's not going to happen, and is that how she feels? Trapped? While they talk I reach in and I take them, the moon pies, still warm in my hands.

I get up before the alarm, before the bus, before Mama is awake and ready to check my hair for the butterfly clips she doesn't like. Last night I waited and took some more of the pies from the very top of the pile, only a few, so Mama wouldn't notice, and zipped them into my backpack. She's too distracted, thinking all the time about Greg and Rebecca. She made me promise not to go see her again, and I did promise. She knew I'd promise. She'd never suspect me to break the promise, but I know I have to.

On a piece of paper I wrote the signs or causes of blue skin. *Impending death.* That, I've underlined. If anyone knows the truth, it will be Audrey, Audrey who's saved the girl twice. Audrey who's always awake.

It takes a long time to walk. When we were younger, I made the walk to Audrey's at least once a day, sometimes twice, sometimes on my bicycle. Then as we got older it was all rides and laziness, one of the reasons my middle is so thick, I guess. When I get to Audrey's, Buck is standing outside by the back of the station wagon. The sun is behind him. He looks bigger, standing there in his sweatshirt with the hood up, not like an eight-year-old anymore.

That's because I'm almost nine, he says when I tell him how big he looks. When I laugh he comes closer and gives me this little smile.

You have some of those pies, don't you? he asks, and then he says, his voice low, *For her?*

I pat him on the hood of his sweatshirt. The station wagon is unlocked. I pull the door open and look inside.

I tell Buck to get us a blanket, the biggest he can find, and then I search for the automatic light for the door and slide it over to off.

Go get Audrey, I say, *and tell her to hurry.*

He stares at me and leans close, putting one hand on my backpack where the pies are.

Only if I can come, too, he says.

Just then Audrey appears behind him and puts her hands on Buck's shoulders. It may just be the light, but she looks wide awake, not tired at all.

He can come, she says. *But she could run again, just like last time. She could head for the lake, and then what?*

I open the backpack and take the moon pies out, hidden in the white napkins I wrapped them in, almost glowing. As I stand there with Buck and Audrey, I realize I'm not worried about dying, not today. We're going to miss the biology test, the one that Greg is probably going to fail, and now so will I.

She won't run, I say. *Not if we feed her.*

But that's not all she eats, Audrey says.

I don't know what Audrey means, but I just nod. Buck and I scrunch down in the backseat and pull the blanket he brought in his backpack over our heads. Audrey goes to get their father. He comes out with his shoulders slumped and slides into the driver's seat. I can see him through the thick blanket, but he doesn't seem to notice us at all. I think about his brain, about its lack of neurotransmitters, about everything it hasn't been doing since he went into the hospital. He looks so sad that his brain has turned against him.

Just out to the lake, Dad, she says to him when he gets behind the wheel. She has the Nerf ball in her hands. *Just you and me at the lake, you and me and the ball. You can play when we get home.*

He just sits there, staring. I feel my breath coming quicker under the blanket and wonder if I'll hyperventilate, if my heart will move into tachycardia right there in the car. Who's to say I won't die?

It's O.K., Buck whispers to me under the blanket. *Audrey will make it O.K. again.*

Buck tells me how Audrey felt when she saved her.

She tells me everything about her at night, he whispers as we huddle under the blanket. *I get into bed with her, and she tells me how she went underwater, and how the girl punched her, right in the face. What I like best is when she tells me how it felt to have her mouth on the blue girl's mouth.*

I ask Buck what else he knows, and he says, *She feels big now. Inside.*

I hear Buck whispering more, but I can't make out the words. Finally Audrey's father starts the car, and I lie under the blanket thinking about what I want the blue girl to know. I unzip the backpack as quietly as I can. Her father drives. Someone is singing. Maybe it's Audrey. I pull one of the moon pies out, unwrapping it as quietly as I can, and then I hold it up against my mouth and whisper into it all the things I want to say.

Libby

THAT NIGHT I FINALLY DREAMED AGAIN, BUT IT was not a relief. Through all this time of not dreaming, I've thought of my mind as a soaked ball that needed to be wrung out to dry. Not a sopping towel or a blanket, but a ball. Not something that could be sent to a dry cleaner or moved through a wash cycle, but something that just needed to be set out in the sun, allowing the liquid to seep out and eventually dry. So it was not a surprise that I dreamed, before waking up to Magda's call about finding Greg and Rebecca on the porch, about the creaking of the wicker sofa.

On top of her, she said on the phone to me. *They didn't see me, and I didn't stop them. I just closed the door. That was wrong, I know, but what kind of mother would I be not to tell you? What kind of friend? That is what I want to know, Libby. What kind of friend would not tell?*

It's not that she wanted to call, she said. She had no desire to bother me at night, on a night when we had no plans to go to the girl, on a night when Ethan had knocked all the pots and pans to the floor and laughed his high-pitched laugh, then threw them, one after another, at the white kitchen wall, now marked up with metal spots.

What kind of a mother am I, is more the point, I said, looking at the wall. Ethan had thrown the pots and then sat on the kitchen floor and rocked back and forth. *Rebecca tells me nothing. Maybe it's because I don't ask.*

Ethan was eating bits of chocolate that I use for the moon pies. I handed him the rest of the bag and just stood watching, doing nothing, as he shoveled in one piece after another.

Good for Ethan, he said, *so good,* and then he cried, the way he does, my broken boy who does things he and no one else understands.

I didn't even know Rebecca was gone.

Go ahead and disappear, I told Jeff the night before when he came in from work at two in the morning. *Do it already. You might as well be gone.*

I told Magda not to tell me anymore, not now, because first I had to get my son into bed, my son who had thrown my pots all over the kitchen and eaten an entire bag of chocolate.

Greg went after her, that boy of mine, Magda said. *Such bad manners and always with the swearing. She ran out with her jacket with that boy of mine chasing after her. Him, always with the chasing. I should have gone after her in the car, not let her walk so far at night.*

She'll be all right, I said. *She knows the way.*

Yes, Magda said, *better than we do,* and we laughed for a minute before she said, *Tomorrow night. Tomorrow night we need to go.*

Yes, yes, I know we need to go, can't she feel how much I know it? But I am behind on my moon pies and have no time for baking. I have a son, crying, with a face filled with chocolate, and a daughter walking home in this small lake town, humiliated in her jacket. A daughter I need right now to help get her brother off the floor and up to bed where he belongs.

We lock him in, it's true. I've talked to Jeff about installing a different alarm with an extra sensor for Ethan's door, since he tripped the first one so many times we had it disconnected. Jeff didn't answer, because that is how Jeff is. Disconnected. Here I am, caging up my own son. But how could I sleep if I let him wander in the night, through the hallway and down the stairs? Before we began locking his door, he went into Rebecca's room, and she guided him back into his bed with the white sheets and the white walls and the white pillows, with even the white moon shining out his window. So now, of course she goes with Greg. What kind of a life has this been for a young girl?

And what about me? Jeff says when I get Ethan off the floor without his help, as always. *What the hell kind of life do you think this is for me?* he says when I tell him my concerns for Rebecca, our daughter so beautiful that all the men's eyes follow her in town. If she's smart she'll keep walking until they can't see her anymore, until she's walked herself straight out of this town, away from all of us, from the girl who swallows our pies and the boy who can't stop touching her.

But she would never leave her brother. This much I know. She loves her brother, who calls to her from behind the locked door, *Becca, Becca, Ethan wants to go. Ethan wants out.*

I get Ethan off the floor and take him upstairs where Jeff is now, home early this night as if to erase the lateness from the night before. When I get Ethan to his room and prepare to lock the door from the outside, I turn him around and tell him, *Say good-night to Dad.*

He looks straight at Jeff with that blank stare of his and laughs.

Ethan goes to bed now, go to bed, Ethan, brush your teeth, Ethan, Ethan, go to bed! Ethan shouts in his cartoon voice.

Yes, I say, and press the fleshy part of his right hand.

It's to make him feel connected to himself again, one of his teachers had taught me. *It's not just that he has trouble making sense of things we take for granted,* she said, *but imagine walking around feeling the way he does, like his head is in one place and his body is in another.*

Wants to rub the hand, he says. *Good boy, Ethan, that's good,* and I say, *Yes, I'll rub the hand, and now Ethan will brush his teeth, yes, good, come now, Ethan is so good, and now Ethan must go to bed.*

When Ethan turns, my two hands still kneading the flesh of his palm, he speaks low in his own voice, the deep voice of the boy who is inside, always locked inside. The boy who only appears as his truest self just when I suspect his truest self is gone.

Good-night, Dad, he says. *Good-night.*

When Jeff doesn't answer, Ethan makes a whimpering sound, the way he does sometimes before a fit or when sounds or lights agitate him.

It's all right, Ethan, I say. *Ethan said good-night.*

I watch him brush his teeth in the careful way he has of being sure not to let the toothpaste touch his lips or tongue, then I take him into the white bedroom and tell him good-night. Before I shut off the light, his eyes are closed, his head on the pillow that he folds over his ears before he begins to rock, slowly, always first left and then right. I close the door and lock it from the outside and lean against it listening for sounds, for any sounds, until I hear Rebecca at the back door.

I cannot let him wander, I say aloud outside his room. *I cannot let this happen.*

It already happened, Rebecca says.

I want to ask her who she is talking about, herself or Ethan, but Ethan is banging, and we are both so tired.

Just go to bed, Mom, she says. *He's not going anywhere tonight, and neither am I.*

I move to hug her but stop myself, because I can see in her eyes she has had enough touching for one night.

In the dream I was playing with Irene's husband, Colin, the two of us throwing a Nerf ball from one to another, back and forth, back and forth. The ball was soft and dry, not soaked as I've imagined, but still I was afraid to drop it.

It's your turn to shoot, Colin said.

He pointed a finger at me and then at the hoop he kept hung over a doorframe.

I tossed the ball back to him. He spun it on one finger and threw it back at me, hard.

I don't want to, I said. I tried to get up from the couch but found my pants soaked through with marshmallow filling.

Please, I said, *I don't want to be the one to shoot.*

You shoot first, Colin said. He placed the ball in the middle of the floor. *Or else there is no more game.*

So I shoot first.

I take the dream as a sign, because how else can anyone take a dream after years of wanting? And what is it that I want from my own husband and Ethan and Rebecca? It used to be that I was a different sort of woman, a woman who could say, *I want this but not that, and this more than anything.* I used to be filled with wanting. I wonder if Rebecca is that way now, the pretty girl in town filled with wanting, the pretty girl who inspires all the wanting. I wonder if that's what my mother wanted for me. I wish she were here to ask, even if the answer disappointed us both. *If I'm going to lock my son in his room,* I think, standing in the dark, with moon pies sealed inside the Ziploc bag that I carry in my tote, *then I am going to be first.*

We're in the dark, under the trees, when I tell them I must be first this time. *It's something I have to do,* I tell Irene and Magda when we get there and stand outside in the dark, with the pies warm and our breath in clouds in front of us. Irene lights a cigarette and offers it to Magda and then to me, but smoke in my mouth and lungs is not one of the things I want. At least I seem to know what I don't want, even if I don't know what it is I do want.

Oh, Libby, Irene says, *we should have known. Always, always, of course. From now on, you should go first.*

Magda touches my hand and tells me how hard it must be for me. *So hard,* she says, *having a son like him. Never mind the foolishness happening with Greg and Rebecca.*

Like him? I ask. As if he has no name. And what does that mean, *like him?* All these years in this town, and still, is this how they think of my son—a boy like him—all of them probably saying their prayers at night in gratitude that they have not been—what is it one of the women from the PTA once said?—burdened. No . . . not burdened . . . saddled, maybe, like a horse. I think of all of the looks I got when I used to take him to the store, before he grew so tall and became harder and harder to hold. Or when the kids were small, out at the lake when they first started to notice he couldn't follow their games, the lake that shimmers now as we stand here, three women with moon pies. *How sad it must be,* I've heard people say, *to have a son "like that."*

Even my mother said it once, that she knew it must be hard on me to have a boy "like that." I forgave her—what else could I do? She was my mother—though I never did forget.

Magda is sorry. It's not that I blame her, or any of them. Not my mother, surely, who cared more for girls, truly, and understood so little. Of course it is sad. It would be a lie to say otherwise. But I will not give in to the sadness.

Brittle is what I am, Magda tells me, the words catching in her voice. *My mama was right about me. I have no softness.*

Look at us, I think. Now we are women like that. We are women with baskets and napkins and tote bags, all for a girl who cannot get out of bed. A girl who seems to drown but still lives. As if we can do something, anything, for such a girl.

But then as we approach the house I think to myself, *Who's to say we can't?*

It's so dark I nearly trip on the steps. I feel Irene's hand fold around my elbow to catch me, and as I reach out to knock, I think of Ethan in the white room alone—asleep, I hope—dreaming whatever it is he dreams.

When he was younger I used to imagine myself tunneling into his head, digging under his skin and cracking through the skull, all without pain. I'd slide inside the blood and pulp of his brain, into the broken synapses. I would tie them together with twine to refasten them. When I could tell I was finished by the synapses lighting up all around me, I'd burrow through the walls of his brain, opening the damaged part so it could get into the spaces where it was clear—because I knew there were spaces that were clear.

As I think about the way I used to imagine myself fixing his brain from the inside, standing there at the door, a feeling moves through me. I realize that all my life I've tried so hard to be clear.

When the old woman finally opens the door and stands there with her hands in her pockets, glaring at us, twisting her pockets into knots, I suddenly know that what I really want is something I can never have.

We're so late, I say to her. Tonight I feel bold, speaking to the old woman for the first time. From the beginning I've let the others speak while I waited. I've spent so many nights that way, waiting for my turn with her.

We are sorry, I say, but the woman does not move away from the door. *We didn't mean to be so late. We know she's hungry. We don't mean to keep her waiting. She must be so hungry by now,* I say. *Please know how sorry we are.*

Finally she steps aside to allow us in. The door to the girl's room is open only a crack so that the light throws one thin slat into the small room where the old woman waits. At first I'm so fixated on the light from the room and the old woman staring at me with her hands in her pockets that I don't hear the sounds. Then suddenly they are upon us, the rumblings of a cough—worse than a cough, the racking sounds of fluid, of a struggle so deep and thick that I nearly drop the moon pies on the floor, tote bag and all.

You send your children, the woman says, and pulls her hand from her pocket. The hand is filled with gravel from the road. I flinch, thinking she may throw it at me, but she shakes it in her hand and begins pacing. *You send your children out to feed her, and now she breathes this way. She chokes on what your children gave her.*

What children? Irene says, but the old woman moves away from us and toward the door, where she paces back and forth, back and forth, the way I have so many nights when Ethan is locked inside his room and bangs against the door.

What shame you should feel, she says, *what shame. I thought you understood how hungry she is, how long she waits. But then the children come, and I see you understand nothing. Now she will not eat. Now she will not eat again.*

The coughing comes again, thick, filled with phlegm. I have a flash of memory of Ethan as a boy with the barking cough of croup. I screamed to Jeff to call the doctor as I sat in the steamy bathroom with him on my lap. He was three or four, maybe, and had yet to speak. Rebecca was still in her crib—that much I can remember. *Like a seal,* the doctor said when he finally arrived. *Unmistakable,* he said. I rocked Ethan back and forth in the steam and then rushed him, like the doctor advised, into the cold night air. The contrast from heat to cold would open up the lungs, the doctor said. Jeff yelled instructions to me from the downstairs telephone. *Don't wake the baby!* I screamed back at him, in those years when we still yelled and screamed, when Jeff still cared enough to be anything but silent. I stood in the backyard in my nightgown and socks, squatting down on the ground and holding Ethan's mouth open with my hands, as if I could force him to suck in the air. My whole body was covered with goose pimples as I stood there, my arms and legs shaking so hard I fell over onto the grass tipped with ice.

Your children come, the old woman goes on, as the coughing gets louder and louder, from a low rumble to a dark wheeze with a scratched intake, and I can feel in my own throat burning. *She is hungry, so she eats what they bring. She eats when I am not here to look out for her. You take so long to come, too long this time, too long.*

Magda and Irene and I look at each other in the dark room and step back from the old woman. She is small but very angry. Furious, even. I hear her knuckles crack inside her pockets.

I don't understand, I say, because I don't. I no longer understand. And this is why I do not dream.

The old woman moves forward and tries to grab one of the moon pies from Magda's linen napkin, but Magda is too quick and raises her arm in the air.

The children, Magda says, holding the napkin high in the air above the woman's head. *Tell me, old woman, what children are you talking about?*

A boy and two girls, says the old woman, pacing now over the rug that looks as if it has been swept far too many times. The longer we stand there, the more clear my sight becomes, until I can make out the swirls of what once must have been color in the rug. Reds, oranges, a dull yellow. Nothing blue.

That boy, Magda says. She lets her arm fall down at her side and nearly falls into one of the chairs. The coughing goes on and on. *That boy of mine.*

At least I know it is not Ethan. I glance at Magda slumped in the wooden chair, defeated, and for once I am glad to have a son "like that." A son who will never touch a girl the way Magda's son touches mine.

Little boy does not go in. He stands at the door. The little boy I do not blame.

Buck? Irene says. *Oh my God, oh, no.*

Little boy does not go in, but the girls, yes, says the old woman in a flurry of hands and breath. She picks something from her teeth and chews on it, then moves toward the door where the light still throws shadows into the room.

Let us try, I say. The cough grows louder and more intense. *Let us try to feed her. She's never refused us before.*

The old woman circles the rug and stares at me, hands moving, always, in the pockets.

Let me try, I say, *just me. I have a boy who is also in a room. I have a boy like her.*

The old woman spits something from her teeth.

No one, she says, moving close enough to me that she is eye level with my breast, *is like her.*

She pulls the door open and waves me in.

Go, she says.

The girl is sitting up against the pillows and stops coughing as soon as I approach. The curtains from the window beside the bed move slowly back and forth, but when I move to pull the window closed, I see it has already been locked and latched. The girl looks bluer, if that's possible. Bluer than the deepest dream. Her skin looks cracked, like it's been splattered with more color than even she can take, and it's clear to me standing there that this is not a condition she has developed but a lifetime of bluish hints that have bit by bit overtaken her. I lift the tote bag onto her bed and pull it open so she can see inside.

There is more to give, I say. *We have not given enough. Surely you must understand how much we want to give.*

She wheezes softly. Her lips part.

Yes, I say. *Good. You understand.*

She closes her mouth at this remark and sniffs the air. I take this as my cue and reach inside the tote bag. Slowly I unwrap it. I slide it out of the Ziploc and pass the pie across to her, allowing the sweet smell to rise in the air between us. I break off a piece, and in my carelessness bits of chocolate float down onto the comforter.

Sorry, I say, as I hold the piece of the moon pie in my fingers and out to her. *Sorry.*

And then the terrible thing happens. Her jaw opens down to her chest, her pink tongue clacks against the roof of her mouth and then drops, and just as I think she can open no wider, her mouth becomes enormous, spewing forth a torrent of white foam. I jump up from the bed as she heaves a stream of filling all over the comforter and the pillows, a bubbling ferment of white that comes and comes until it stops.

Rebecca

ETHAN IS GONE.

I knew it before anyone else. I could feel it.

As soon as I woke up, I remembered the weight of Greg on top of me on the couch on his porch and the smell of vanilla and chocolate, and inside my head I knew—Ethan got out. I knew before my mother screamed and started running through the house, before all the phone calls to my father at work, who never picked up the phone. I was still dialing his number over and over when Audrey and Caroline and Magda and Greg and Buck showed up and scoured the yard, calling his name to the trees beyond the white fence. I was sitting with the telephone, on the kitchen floor, with my knees up to my chest, scraping chocolate off the floor.

Hang up, Mom said. *That sonofabitch.*

Greg came in and didn't say fuck once, realizing, I guess, that this was not the time to say it. He put his arm around me and started stroking my hair and saying things about not worrying and taking care of me, and even something about love. I didn't want to hear any of it, not then, but still I let him say it, because I thought my own father didn't care whether we were here or not, me or Ethan, and for a minute I felt like smashing the phone on the floor so he'd have to pick up the pieces to keep the house white, perfect, without color. They were all out there looking while I sat on the floor, just letting Greg stroke my hair while low sounds started coming out of me—not like crying, exactly, maybe crying without tears. My face stayed dry, but the sounds still came.

Now the cop they called is here and wants to talk to me. Mom comes into the kitchen and opens the cabinets under the sink, calling, *Ethan? Where is Ethan?* like the games of hide-and-seek we used to play when he was little, which he never understood because he'd always jump out and yell, *Ethan is here!*

I push Greg away, get up, and walk over to my mom. I bend down to try to help her up, but she feels thick, weighted down, stuck to the floor. When I try to pull her up, her pants make a squishing sound.

I don't blame you, she says. *I want you to know I don't blame you,* and then I feel that sound coming out of me again, and I say, *Blame me for what?*

For any of it, she says. *It's not your fault that you went.*

The cop starts up with the questions while I lean against the counter.

All the questions. There have always been so many questions about Ethan. *Why does he talk that way? Why are his ears flat? He's retarded, right? What does it feel like, having a brother who bangs his head and can't do much of anything for himself?* But the questions I have are about the girl. The girl out trying to drown herself in the lake. *Why doesn't he ask about her?* I wonder. Then I realize that he doesn't know.

I tell the cop I did not let my brother out. That is the truth. *Other nights, yes,* I say, *there are times when I've let him out of the room because the banging gets to be too much and because I have to sleep, I have school.* Didn't this guy ever go to school? *But when I've let him out of his room, I've kept him in my room with me, where he buries his head in my beanbag chair and falls asleep face down.* The cop says he never had a brother like mine, but he imagines it would be hard. He's seen my brother in the car with my mother or sometimes at the store with us. He imagines there's a lot of strain, he says.

Ethan has problems, I say. *A disability. He has something called fragile X. Do you know what fragile X is, officer?* I say, because I feel that burning in my stomach that I get when people talk about my brother like this.

There are lots of kids like Ethan, I say. *They live everywhere, not just in this stupid lake town. He's not the only one.*

And then I almost say, *And how would you feel if someday you and your bitch wife*—and I don't know why I even think this guy's wife is a bitch when I've never seen the guy before, and why would I care about his wife, and maybe his wife is soulful and kind, the way my mother used to be, but still I want to call her a bitch for some reason—*had a kid like Ethan? How would you feel then having a kid who couldn't understand you or write his own name or be left alone at all at eighteen?*

Or worse, I want to say, as he stands there with his pad and pencil while Magda and Irene and Audrey and Caroline are all out there calling for him. *How would you feel if you had a kid that was blue? A kid like her?*

I'm about to say this when all of a sudden I hear Audrey yell from the back door, *Mom, Jesus, Mom, where's Buck?*

Now Buck is gone, too. Buck is not in the yard or in the car or hiding under the cabinets where my mother is still pulling pots. Buck is not there, Buck is somewhere else, and though I can't think about it now, I know I'm going to be wondering for a long time just what happened last night after I let Greg push himself into me on the couch, and just what our mothers were doing last night with their moon pies. They were gone for a very long time, longer than they'd ever been gone before, and I'm going to be wondering how two of those mothers let their sons go missing without even noticing they were gone.

But I can't think about that now. There's no time now. Now I have to get Audrey alone.

Before the cop can get to Irene and the screaming Audrey, who's shaking her mother by the arms at the back door while Magda tries to pull her off, he asks me where I was last night, if I can prove where I was, because they have to think that maybe, just as a possibility, Ethan was taken.

I turn to him, and I want to say, *I was with my boyfriend. His mother caught us. She opened the door and saw. I know she did. Go ahead and ask them all,* but I don't. I stand there looking at the cop and at Greg, who says nothing, not even fuck.

I move away from the cop, whose attention is on Irene now anyway, and I push Greg away as he tries to grab me around the waist and hold me. *It's not that the holding isn't nice,* I want to say, *but not now, Jesus, not now,* but what comes out is me telling him, *Get the fuck off me, Greg, and tell the officer the fucking truth.*

I was with Rebecca, he says. No fucks. I struggle to get across the room to Audrey, who's squeezing her mother's arms, her face whiter than I've ever seen it. She's whiter than anything naturally white, whiter than the kitchen with the white walls and the white counter and all the white things that help Ethan feel safe. But this is one shade of white I've never seen.

What if she did it? I say to Audrey, as I pull her over to the space between the kitchen and the upstairs landing. *What if she took him?*

Who? Caroline asks. I didn't see her coming up, and for a minute I think of staying quiet, but then I see a look pass between Caroline and Audrey, and I know they've been out there. The two of them. Without me.

Her, I say, and then under my breath, *Why didn't you ask me to go?*

Audrey moves between us and says, *O.K., O.K., not now. You're right, O.K.? There was no time. It was Caroline's idea, and we made my dad drive. We shouldn't have. We shouldn't have left you out.*

Our mothers are calling their names, Buck, Ethan, over and over. They draw out the sounds with their hands cupped over their mouths. The cop is trying to keep them quiet, but they just keep calling and calling and calling. Calling for the boys, all except Greg, who stands in the corner with his hands in his pockets with no one to touch.

We never should have taken Buck, either, Audrey says. *But he begged. Him and those dreams.* She looks down at her sneakers and adds, *I thought I could make them stop.*

Her blond hair hangs over her face, and I know she's crying. I can see it in everything, her shoulders, her hands. When Ethan cries, he rolls his hands. I look down at Audrey's freckled hands and think of my brother's turning and turning, and how he hates hands, hands that touch, hands that squeeze, hands in front of his face, hands too big, hands too small. As I think about my brother and how he hates hands, for some reason I realize what's happened. They've gone out there, they've gone to see her.

You don't think . . . Caroline says.

It's the first time Caroline and I have looked at each other in a long time, maybe since that day out at the lake when we saw her drowning and Audrey saved her. Before we thought of stealing cars and our moms went crazy making all those moon pies.

Oh, yeah, I say. *I do think.*

We have to get the cop to go, I whisper to Audrey, and she nods and wipes her nose with the back of her hand. She knows that if they're out there with the blue girl, we can't let the cop see her, or Buck and Ethan. Who knows what a cop would do to them?

She tried to do it while we were out there, Audrey says, *right before we left. She does it all the time. I heard the old lady say it. Every day she runs for the lake and throws herself in. Then everything is wet, the old lady said, the bed, the covers, everything.*

It was really hard to get her out, Audrey says, almost to herself. *I almost didn't make it.*

Greg, do something already, don't just stand there, Caroline says. *Go get rid of the cop.*

We move over to the door and watch as Greg starts talking to the cop with his hands moving all the time. He points down the road toward the school where Ethan goes in his yellow bus. I watch the cop talking into his radio as he drives away and our mothers stand there. Magda has her arms around the two of them, my mother and Irene, and when I look over at Greg, I think maybe it wasn't so bad out on the porch. Maybe I can feel something for him, I think, if we can get them back, Ethan and Buck, and her, the girl who tries over and over to drown herself.

We take my mother's van. It's so much easier than I thought, getting our mothers to listen to us once Audrey tells them that we think Buck and Ethan went out there, that the girl ate the moon pies that they brought, her and Caroline. *Stole,* Audrey says, but she doesn't say she's sorry. She tells our mothers that the girl ran into the lake again and that she pulled her out. Again.

I took Buck with me, Ma, she says, *because he begged.*

Irene doesn't answer.

I sit in the back between Audrey and Caroline. We keep the windows open so we can see the sides of the road. We made Greg stay behind in case they come back while we're gone. By the time we left, Greg's father had shown up and stood in the yard with Greg. I could see he was confused. His father doesn't say or do much, either, but at least he shows up. Greg kissed me in front of his father, but I wasn't embarrassed. I told Greg to keep trying my own father until he picked up the phone.

Forget about your dad, Greg's dad said to me, leaning in to say it low as I got into the car. *Don't worry about your dad,* he said. *Just find your brother and that blue whatever-she-is.*

I didn't think any of them knew, any of the dads, but now I see I was wrong. We were stealing cars, our mothers were making moon pies, we all thought nobody else knew, but maybe the dads knew all along. There's no time to worry about what they know. There's only Ethan, Ethan afraid of hands and things not white, and little Buck, who has somehow managed to walk all the way out to the lake to find the blue girl.

It's where he has to be. I know it before we can even get there.

As we drive I feel Audrey's hair whip against me. I close my mouth against the wind and let her hair and mine sting my cheeks and lips. When we get close, Audrey and Caroline lean back and tell me about the night they went out there without me, how they convinced Audrey's father to drive.

Buck and I stayed under the blanket, Caroline says, *until we heard the old lady at the door, and she started saying such terrible things about our mothers. She said they were fools, unkind, and that they wanted the girl to starve.*

I fed her, Audrey says, as we pull down the gravel road to the grove of trees that leads to the lake. *She ate all the moon pies we had.*

Gravel sprays up through the windows and hits me in the face. I see the outline of the lake beyond the trees as Audrey keeps talking.

Then, as soon as she was done, she ran for the water and jumped in. I was almost too tired to pull her out.

Audrey turns to look at me and pulls her hair away from her face. She looks so tired.

She looked so sad, Audrey says, *like she couldn't believe I'd pulled her out again. Just so, so sad.*

We pull in closer to the lake, and there is Ethan, standing waist-deep in the water. My mother screams. I don't know who tramples over me, Audrey or Caroline, but the next thing I know I am down on the ground with my knees in the gravel. Somebody pulls me up—Magda, I think—and I feel the cuts burning as I run to the water's edge.

I try to look for my mother, but everyone is in front of me, all of their bodies keeping me from seeing past them, from seeing where Ethan is. I brush off my legs and think about how I left him last night when he was still banging, that I got up and went to bed without letting him follow me the way I usually do when he won't settle down. I think about how I lay in bed waiting for my mother to get home, how I must have fallen asleep to his sounds.

Only when I get close enough can I see that Ethan is holding the blue girl in his arms. The water comes up to his waist. He has one arm under her neck and one under her legs. Her head hangs back like a doll's, the neck and face and hands, all of it blue. Even from here I can see she's not breathing.

Buck stands by the far side of the lake. Irene shrieks his name. He runs toward Audrey and hugs her hard around the waist, so hard she stumbles.

Ethan! I call. *Ethan's O.K. now. Ethan's going to be O.K.*

He starts to rock back and forth in the water, the girl's blue arms sinking deeper as he sways. I watch as Audrey peels Buck's arms from around her waist and wades into the water in her jeans and sneakers. Caroline grabs for Audrey, but Audrey shrugs her off and moves forward until the water reaches her knees. She raises both arms above her head, about to dive in, when Buck splashes into the water and pulls her back.

No, Audrey, he says. *The old lady said no, remember?*

He points toward the gravel road where the old lady stands with her hands on her hips and shakes her head at us.

See? Buck says.

Audrey stops. I find my mother and take her hand, and Caroline takes Magda's, and Audrey and Buck take each of Irene's. Together we move a bit farther into the water, so cold it makes my breath stop. I look back at the old lady, shaking her head no, and then I look out at Ethan there in the lake. From where I stand, with the light hitting him just this way, he looks the way he was meant to look, I think, without his fragile X. His face looks shorter and less pointed, his ears not so flat.

Becca? he says. *Ethan's O.K. now. Ethan's O.K. You see, Becca? Here's Ethan, here he is. Ethan's O.K.*

My mother and I turn to look at each other. She squeezes my hand and whispers for me to say it.

That's right, I call out to him. *Ethan's O.K. now. Ethan's O.K.* And then, *Blue girl is O.K. now, Ethan.*

He pauses for a minute and stands there. The girl's blue skin glows against the white glare of the sun. He laughs his cartoon laugh and then stops, and when he does, he opens his arms and lets her go.

Irene

I SIT ON THE PORCH WITH THE WINDOWS OPEN AND SING along with the trees. I am not sure that what I hear is singing, exactly, but singing is what it seems to be, and singing is what I do. I sing in a voice so soft I can hardly hear my own words or feel my breath that presses down in my chest. I sit with a blanket wrapped around my shoulders and try hard to listen, as my mother had always told me, and to let my voice carry on.

If you listen hard enough, Irene, my mother used to say when I was a girl not much younger than Audrey, *you will hear all of the songs, every one.*

I try to remember the words she taught me, the songs she sang to me when I was a little girl afraid to sleep in a bed too large, when I wanted to be something other than my own frightened self. What was it that frightened me back then, when we lived in this town by the lake, when the woods were not so dark, the lake shining, the summer people not coming in yet to crowd all that had been ours? Had I heard another girl in the night, another girl who coughed and turned blue from wanting? Had I known then, as a child, that I would live in this town with a girl who would do too much saving and a boy too young for dreams and a husband who played meaningless games? Had I actually known all of that back then, that one day I would be this kind of woman?

Perhaps I had. Perhaps I had known all of it then. Perhaps we all know what will become of us, that one day we will have children who do not or cannot follow what we say, that what seems broken is in fact strongest. Perhaps we know then that one day we will have to release what we are tired of feeding and caring for, when the song of the trees is all we can hope to hear.

I lie down on the couch and let the breeze from the windows blow all around me and think of the girl sinking down into the water with her eyes closed, not open as they'd been all the other times she had been saved.

She was so tired, Mom, is all, Audrey said the night Ethan let her go into the lake. *She was just so very, very tired.*

I didn't know whether Audrey meant the blue girl or herself, or both of them. After all that had happened, I could not bring myself to ask.

The girl had disappeared into the water that glittered in the sun, and Rebecca had led Ethan back to the shore and wrapped him in blankets from the trunk of the car. As he shivered and rocked, Buck knelt down beside him and wrapped his arms around this eighteen-year-old boy who will never grow up. He told Buck in a quiet voice that Ethan was O.K. now, Ethan was going to be O.K., and Ethan leaned his head against Buck's and kept it there.

That night, I thought about our last night out in the woods with the girl, how the old woman wiped the girl's face with a cloth soaked in water from the lake and told us not to come to her again.

We were only trying to help, we said. *Can't you see?* We were good mothers, most of the time, we said, even if we had been distracted while we made the pies and fed the girl. Why couldn't the old woman see that it pained us to see the girl in such a state? Surely she must have known that we meant the girl no harm.

Your children came, the old woman said, as she sopped up more lake water with the cloth and wiped the girl's mouth and forehead. *Only you and only at night is what I said.* The smell of the lake water had filled the room. *At night she cries while you are in your homes baking. How can you not hear the crying? How can you not listen? She gets out of the bed from all the waiting to throw herself in, and only I am here to stop her.*

The droplets rained down into the basin and sent out tiny ripples that spread slowly, rings of water moving ever so slowly across the surface until they collided and burst all at once.

Maybe now it is time, the old woman said.

Time for what? Libby asked, but the old woman did not answer.

The girl moved in the bed, the covers rustling, and turned to look at me from the pillow.

Irene, Magda said, and then Libby, too. *Look. She wants Irene.*

The old woman slapped the cloth into my hand and clomped into the outer room where she began pacing. All night long she paced, murmuring to herself and moving her hands in the pockets of her apron. Every few circles she stopped and peered in, then shook her head and began pacing again.

I spent a long time looking at the girl before pressing the cloth against her forehead, down over her cheeks, her mouth that had stopped dribbling moon pie filling. Magda moved the lamp from the dresser next to the girl's bed, and together we stood over her, trying to look as closely as we could at the skin that appeared to become bluer as the night wore on.

I looked at her and searched my mind for the palette of colors I wished I had in front of me. I wished I could paint her there, with the light throwing itself over her dark shoulders and pulsating throat. I thought that if I were to spend the rest of my life trying to mix the precise color of her skin, and if I were to tell this story to Audrey or Buck or their children someday, I would never find the right word to say how blue she really was. A dark turquoise, deeper than any indigo. The violet swirl of the sky just before dark or of ink spilled and left to dry. It was as if her skin was waging a battle against its own blueness, and was losing.

She settled back against the pillows and sighed, a sigh filled with longing and phlegm. The edges of her lips were crusted over with what appeared to be purple scabs. I blotted them, first with the cloth and then with my finger.

When I touched her lips, I nearly flinched from the heat. I raised my hand in a kind of offering and then pressed the back of it to her forehead, her cheeks. Her skin nearly crackled with fever.

Are you sick? I whispered, not wanting the old woman to hear. *Do you feel sick?*

The girl's eyes closed. She nodded, her head moving up and down, up and down.

What had the children fed her? I wondered as I stood beside the bed. Perhaps the old woman was right. Perhaps they were responsible for the froth of white filling and the girl's fevered skin. Whatever they gave her had come from us, from Magda and Libby and me. Maybe all of our secrets had finally taken a toll on this girl who had come from the lake one day only to eventually drown for good. Had we done nothing but keep her alive for our own sake, and not for hers?

All night we took turns giving her sips of water. Magda and Libby made several trips down the road to the lake. Magda cupped the water in her hands and let the drops fall over the girl's closed eyes and open mouth while Libby passed the washcloth up and down her arms, arms so dark that there were no visible veins. Finally, when her skin seemed to cool, and she no longer held her mouth open for water to sip, we got in to our cars and drove home without saying good-bye.

It was not really a surprise when the phone rang with the news that Ethan was gone. This is the kind of distraction the girl brought into our lives, and so that night, after Ethan opened his arms and let her sink down into the lake, I wondered what kind of person I may have become that I would call such a thing relief.

It is very late as I close the windows against the sounds of the trees. I have grown tired of listening, tired of trying to please my mother who wanted me to have a life of singing, tired of the blue girl who lived among the trees and ate our moon pies again and again. Last night, as the sun was setting, we watched the old woman disappear into the trees without a word. We kissed each other's cheeks and hugged each of the children, even Ethan, who hates hands and touch, even he leaned in, with his arms stiff, and allowed each of us to embrace him. I pulled away in the station wagon, the first to go. By the time we reached home, Buck had fallen asleep in the backseat. Audrey lifted him in her arms and carried him to his bedroom while I followed with freshly washed blankets, and pressed my face into his hair, which still smelled like the lake.

I just want to go to bed, Mom, Audrey said, *even though I know you want to talk.*

Yes, of course, I said. *Talking can wait. You haven't slept in so long.*

I watched as she peeled off the jeans and socks she'd worn in the lake in her last attempt to save the girl. I watched as she pulled the covers up to her chin and closed her eyes, then listened for the rhythmic breathing and slight whistle through her nose that always indicated she was in a deep sleep, ever since she was a baby. It was that whistle that had made me think of singing, that whistle that kept me sitting on the porch, singing in a low voice while I wondered about the girl who had sunk down into the water, down deeper than any of us will ever go.

After I close the windows on the porch and get onto the cot in the guestroom, where I have been sleeping ever since Colin first convinced himself the television would explode, I realize I have not checked on Colin since the morning, when the phone calls began, telling us Ethan had gone missing. Colin had spoken to me that morning. He hadn't in weeks, not in sentences, not with the kind of meaning that happens between husbands and wives, even in marriages strained by children, illness, or the distraction of baking. When Audrey explained to him that we had to leave right away, he actually seemed to understand, though not at first.

Please, Dad, she said, *put down your ball and listen for a minute. Ethan's helpless. He gets locked in his bedroom at night, and he got out. He can't be let out alone.*

I remember Colin turning to me and saying, *What a terrible thing it must be for him to be locked up like that.*

I hadn't answered then, but I think I can now. I pad into the living room and find Colin just sitting, holding his Nerf ball. He is not playing a game. He is looking first at the television and then at the ball and then back at the television again.

The boy is all right, I say. I sit down next to him on the sofa. He does not try to move away from me. *This morning you said how hard it must be, and you are right, Colin. It is hard.*

He lays the ball down in the space between us.

Yes, he says. *It is.*

Six months later, I discover that Colin is gone. It is spring, that time when we are still just a town that happens to have a lake, a town that will change with the arrival of the summer people who take up residence in the cottages along the lakeshore and bring with them children in matching bathing suits and sand toys and chairs and towels. I tell no one. Audrey has only begun to sleep again, and she and Caroline and Rebecca laugh during the evenings in Audrey's room. Every Thursday Buck and I drive to Libby's, where he and Ethan sit and watch cartoons. Libby's husband works late most nights, and she takes comfort in the bits of dreams she has begun to have again. Sometimes she even tells them to me. Rebecca and Greg continue to meet, but never on Magda's porch.

We talk about many things, the three of us, but never about that last day at the lake. It is as if we are afraid that if we start talking, we might never be able to stop.

I am alone in the house when I find the basketball hoop removed from its place over the door and the Nerf ball left sitting on the living room sofa, the foam ball pecked as if by birds. Just before I find the ball, I had planned to go out to the lake for the first time since the day we watched her float out there, down and away from us. At times I wonder whether we will find her one day, spread out on the lake water with her skin throwing blue shadows over the sun. If she does surface, will we leave her there or try to fish her out? I don't know the answers, but I do miss the smell of the moon pies from time to time, the baking and feeding, the feeling of cleanliness in my hand the day she lapped at the bits of marshmallow and chocolate I had made for her.

I find the note folded on the front seat of the car. I unfold it slowly and hold my breath, thinking of what I might say to the children when they come home, when they ask about their father, who stopped playing his games and left behind the television he feared would explode.

I stand there with the note pressed to my chest. I don't call the police or the hospital, or drive out to the lake, not yet. I go back inside the house and pick up the Nerf ball he left behind on the couch. When I lift it, I see a glint of silver stuffed into the space between the seat and the back of the couch. I reach in with my hand to dig it out and find a stale moon pie, one I must have made long ago, wrapped in foil, waiting to be eaten.

TELL THE WORLD THIS BOOK WAS
GOOD
BAD
SO-SO

ACKNOWLEDGMENTS

No book is written in a vacuum, and I offer my gratitude to the following people and places for time, encouragement, and solace:

to the various editors, anthologies, and magazines for space and attention to various portions of this novel;

to the Virginia Center for the Creative Arts for gloriously uninterrupted time;

to all of the folks at Coffee House Press, especially to Chris Fischbach, Caroline Casey, Amelia Foster, and Molly Fuller, who have helped shepherd this novel through to the end;

to the "Lesley Posse" current students and alum, and to the Lesley faculty who heard early versions of this novel and offered such generous cheering on when I needed it most;

to all of my Goddard people;

to the literary folk I'm lucky to call such fine friends: Alison McGhee, Judith Dupré, Rachel Kadish, Erin Belieu, Tony Eprile, and Chris Lynch, and of course to Cate Marvin;

to Michael, and to our children, Ella and Zachariah, who did not exist at the time of this novel's conception, hard as that seems now to imagine;

to all of the parents and all of the children with special needs who walk this path we walk;

to my father, who gave me gifts too many to enumerate, and whose strength and courage sustain me still;

to my beautiful mother, who was with me for most of the writing of this book, who watched my kids since they were babies so that I could write. There will never be enough words to say how much I thank you, love you, miss you;

to Allan Kornblum for the phone call in 1993 that changed everything, and for the vision and dedication that challenged and bettered all of the novels I had the privilege to work on with him. You are missed, friend.

FUNDER ACKNOWLEDGMENTS

Coffee House Press is an independent, nonprofit literary publisher. All of our books, including the one in your hands, are made possible through the generous support of grants and donations from corporate giving programs, state and federal support, family foundations, and the many individuals that believe in the transformational power of literature. We receive major operating support from Amazon, the Bush Foundation, the McKnight Foundation, and Target. This activity is made possible by the voters of Minnesota through a Minnesota State Arts Board Operating Support grant, thanks to a legislative appropriation from the arts and cultural heritage fund. Our publishing program is also supported in part by the Jerome Foundation and an award from the National Endowment for the Arts. To find out more about how NEA grants impact individuals and communities, visit www.arts.gov.

Coffee House Press receives additional support from many anonymous donors; the Alexander Family Fund; the Archer Bondarenko Munificence Fund; the Elmer L. & Eleanor J. Andersen Foundation; the David & Mary Anderson Family Foundation; the E. Thomas Binger & Rebecca Rand Fund of the Minneapolis Foundation; the Patrick & Aimee Butler Family Foundation; the Buuck Family Foundation; the Carolyn Foundation; the Dorsey & Whitney Foundation; Fredrikson & Byron, P.A.; the Lenfestey Family Foundation; the Mead Witter

Foundation; the Schwab Charitable Fund; Schwegman, Lundberg & Woessner, P.A.; Penguin Group; the Private Client Reserve of US Bank; VSA Minnesota for the Metropolitan Regional Arts Council; the Archie D. & Bertha H. Walker Foundation; the Wells Fargo Foundation of Minnesota; and the Woessner Freeman Family Foundation.

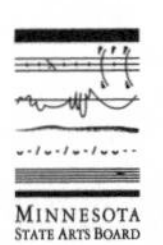

amazon.com

THE McKNIGHT FOUNDATION

THE PUBLISHER'S CIRCLE OF COFFEE HOUSE PRESS

Publisher's Circle members make significant contributions to Coffee House Press's annual giving campaign. Understanding that a strong financial base is necessary for the press to meet the challenges and opportunities that arise each year, this group plays a crucial part in the success of our mission.

"Coffee House Press believes that American literature should be as diverse as America itself. Known for consistently championing authors whose work challenges cultural and aesthetic norms, we believe their books deserve space in the marketplace of ideas. Publishing literature has never been an easy business, and publishing literature that truly takes risks is a cause we believe is worthy of significant support. We ask you to join us today in helping to ensure the future of Coffee House Press."

—THE PUBLISHER'S CIRCLE MEMBERS
OF COFFEE HOUSE PRESS

Publisher's Circle Members include: many anonymous donors, Mr. & Mrs. Rand L. Alexander, Suzanne Allen, Patricia Beithon, Bill Berkson & Connie Lewallen, Robert & Gail Buuck, Claire Casey, Louise Copeland, Jane Dalrymple-Hollo, Mary Ebert & Paul Stembler, Chris Fischbach & Katie Dublinski, Katharine Freeman, Sally French, Jocelyn Hale & Glenn Miller, Jeffrey

Hom, Kenneth & Susan Kahn, Kenneth Koch Literary Estate, Stephen & Isabel Keating, Allan & Cinda Kornblum, Leslie Larson Maheras, Jim & Susan Lenfestey, Sarah Lutman & Rob Rudolph, Carol & Aaron Mack, George Mack, Joshua Mack, Gillian McCain, Mary & Malcolm McDermid, Sjur Midness & Briar Andresen, Peter Nelson & Jennifer Swenson, Marc Porter & James Hennessy, the Rehael Fund-Roger Hale & Nor Hall of the Minneapolis Foundation, Jeffrey Sugerman & Sarah Schultz, Nan Swid, Patricia Tilton, Stu Wilson & Melissa Barker, Warren D. Woessner & Iris C. Freeman, and Margaret & Angus Wurtele.

For more information about the Publisher's Circle and other ways to support Coffee House Press books, authors, and activities, please visit www.coffeehousepress.org/support or contact us at: info@coffeehousepress.org.

ALLAN KORNBLUM, 1949—2014

Vision is about looking at the world and seeing not what it is, but what it could be. Allan Kornblum's vision and leadership created Coffee House Press. To celebrate his legacy, every book we publish in 2015 will be in his memory.

The Blue Girl was designed at Coffee House Press,
in the historic Grain Belt Brewery's Bottling House
near downtown Minneapolis. The text is set in
Spectrum MT with Glamor used as display.